ETHAN

The Surprise Brides Book 4

BY SYLVIA MCDANIEL

Books by Sylvia McDaniel

Contemporary Romance

Standalones
The Reluctant Santa
My Sister's Boyfriend
The Wanted Bride
The Relationship Coach
Her Christmas Lie
Secrets, Lies, and Online Dating
Paying for the Past
Cupid's Revenge

Anthologies
Kisses, Laughter & Love
Christmas with you

Collaborative Series

Magic, New Mexico
Touch of Decadence

Western Historicals

Standalones
A Hero's Heart
A Scarlet Bride
Second Chance Cowboy

The Cuvier Women
Wronged
Betrayed
Beguiled

Lipstick and Lead
Desperate
Deadly
Dangerous
Daring
Determined
Deceived

Scandalous Suffragettes
Abigail
Bella
Callie
Faith

The Burnett Brides
The Rancher Takes a Bride
The Outlaw Takes a Bride
The Marshal Takes a Bride
The Christmas Bride

Anthologies
Wild Western Women
Courting the West
Wild Western Women Ride Again

Collaborative Series

The Surprise Brides
Ethan

American Mail Order Brides
Katie

Ethan
Published by Virtual Bookseller

Cover Design by RomCon
http://www.romcon.com/book-cover-design-custom

Edited by Andrea Dickinson
http://www.qualitybookservices.com/

Formatted by Laurelle Procter
laurelleprocter@gmail.com

Short Description: Beth Worthington defies her father's plans to marry her off by choosing to become a mail-order bride with no intention of staying married to her unknown suitor.

ISBN: 978-1-942608-59-2 (paperback)
ISBN: 978-1-942608-06-6 (e-book)

{Victorian Historical Romance – Fiction}
{Holiday Romance – Fiction}

www.SylviaMcDaniel.com

Synopsis

Beth Worthington finds herself racing from a wealthy older groom into the arms of a stranger when she defies an attempt by her father to marry her off. Instead, she takes matters into her own hands and agrees to become a mail-order bride with no intention of staying married to her unknown suitor.

Ethan Fraser is shocked when he discovers his mother ordered him a bride. To save the innocent girl's reputation, he goes through with the wedding. What he doesn't expect is for his innocent bride to have plans of her own – that don't happen to include him.

When an unexpected snowstorm traps the two together she fights the unwanted attraction and the way of life he has to offer.

Table of Contents

Chapter One

Angel Springs, Colorado, October 1880

Proving he was a man was easy on the Circle F ranch, except when it came to his family. None of them wanted to accept that at the age of twenty-two, the youngest of the four boys had grown up. Not his brothers or his mother, his father had been buried when he was just a boy, but in some ways, Ethan Fraser felt older than his brothers.

Jamie Fraser looked northward. "Snow's coming down fast and thick for this early. Gonna be a hard winter."

Gideon threw the corral gate closed. "Pete better hurry back or he'll be stuck in town with our supplies."

Ethan was certain that Pete, their ranch hand, wouldn't waste any time getting back to the ranch to get out of the cold. The trip had seemed unnecessary and he'd wondered what his mother's urgent need was that she'd send their best ranch hand out into the snow to town.

Caleb turned up his collar. "I'm heading to the house. I don't aim to stand around waiting on Pete, no matter what Mama says."

Jamie shot him a stony stare. "She doesn't ask much of us. Won't kill you to hold off on your carousing for a couple of hours. Besides, you can't head into town in this weather."

Ethan laughed and nudged Caleb. "He doesn't have to. Has himself a sweet little gal stashed at his house."

Caleb pushed at Ethan's chest and sent him tumbling onto the snowy ground. Anger rose up inside Ethan faster than a charging bull. He'd been telling Caleb for days this wasn't a good idea, but as usual, his brother wouldn't listen.

"Keep your mouth shut, little brother. Nobody's business but mine."

Ethan hopped up, and Jamie stopped him before he tackled Caleb. Not that he wanted to hurt his brother, but he got tired of his bossiness. Of all his brothers, Caleb was the one who he worried about the most. The man was running from a demon by chasing every skirt available in town.

"Settle down. We have more important things to do than wrestle in the snow," Jamie scolded his brothers.

The jingle of sleigh bells interrupted their quarrel. Finally, they could unload the wagon and go inside where it was warm.

His mother came out onto the porch and watched the wagon with the skids attached coming up the drive.

"Let's go stand with Mama," Jamie told his brothers, and they trudged through the knee-high snow to their mother's side.

Something was up. An uneasy tingly feeling crept along Ethan's spine. Whatever it was, from Jamie's frowning expression, his older brother knew what was going on.

Gideon craned his neck. "Looks like Pete's got passengers. Who'd be coming here in this weather? You expecting anyone, Mama?"

She straightened. "As a matter of fact, I am. I'd appreciate you boys staying right here with me. I have something important to say to you in a few minutes."

What was she hiding? There was something on that wagon making her act suspicious. If his mother was involved, it probably meant bad news for all of them.

Ethan caught sight of the passengers coming up the drive—four women.

Frowning, Jamie turned to his mother. "Mama, what have you done?"

She crossed her arms over her chest. "What needed doing. Now you get on and help Pete unload the girls' belongings. He doesn't need to do all the work by himself."

Jamie called over his shoulder, "Come on, boys. Lend a hand."

Caleb stepped up beside Jamie. "What's going on?"

"We have to get these women and their belongings inside, so Pete can put up the horses. Mama will explain then," Jamie said shaking his head, clearly frustrated. Their mother had meddled once again.

Ethan gazed at the women, so bundled up he couldn't see more than their eyes and nose. He watched Jamie help each woman down from the wagon and gesture for her to go inside. The last lady was a statuesque brunette who raised her brows and glanced around in a haughty manner as she entered the house.

As he lifted a heavy trunk and carried it indoors, Ethan wasn't certain of what was going on, but four young women with their belongings had just arrived at the ranch. For months, his overbearing mother had been harping on her sons to find women and marry. It appeared she'd taken matters into her own hands and found them brides. Mail-order brides, if he was guessing correctly.

Well, his lady was in for a surprise. He wasn't going to marry the girl.

Helping his brothers, they carried the trunks in until they had the sleigh emptied of women, luggage, and supplies. Pete raised his eyebrows and hopped into the sleigh like his tail was on fire. With a flick of the reins, he headed toward the barn.

Inside the house, the parlor was a flurry of wraps being removed and females chattering. Four women huddled near the fireplace, gazing at the men, their eyes full of curiosity. Each woman was different, but the pretty brunette who stood off to the side drew Ethan's attention. She looked like she'd stepped out of a high society tea, in her fancy coat, fur lined muffler and gloves. The other women's clothing was ordinary, but this woman obviously could afford better quality fashion than the other young ladies. Fashion that had no place on a working ranch.

Milly, the Fraser's cook, set down a tray holding cups of hot chocolate and a plate of cookies. "One of you boys help me get the rest of the mugs, instead of lollygagging. I can only carry so much, you know."

Gideon followed the cook into the kitchen and returned with another tray. "Mama, I believe we deserve introductions and an explanation."

Ethan sat back and watched the goings-on, his stomach clenched in a knot. The brunette, standing off by herself, observed her surroundings like a trail boss surveying his herd. Her coat was made of the finest fabric, and there was an air about her that spoke of old money.

Attempting a smile, Mama licked her lips and gestured toward the men waiting expectantly. "Ladies, these are your grooms."

Ethan fought against his pride, wanting to walk out the door, climb on his horse, and ride to town. This time his mother had really overstepped her bounds.

Caleb reacted first. "What the hell?" He nodded to the women. "Excuse me, ladies." Lowering his voice, he leaned toward his mother. "I hope this is a joke of some kind, and you're not serious."

Ethan stared at the women who looked at each other like they wanted to run but had nowhere to go.

His mother straightened her shoulders and narrowed her eyes at her sons. "Now boys, you each promised me you'd marry someday, but you never did anything toward keeping your word. I decided this was a good time to help you by finding you wives. These ladies have come all the way from Chicago."

Fiona Fraser turned toward the women. After a glance at the photos she held, she took a willowy blonde by the hand and led her across the floor. "Olivia, this is Jamie, my oldest at thirty-two and your groom-to-be. Jamie, Olivia has been a schoolteacher."

Ethan understood why she'd chosen a schoolteacher for Jamie, as he had two children. But what kind of woman did she think Ethan needed?

The remaining three were pretty, but not whom he would have picked to marry.

Next Mama took Caleb by the hand and led him to a brown-eyed woman with black hair. "Lillian, meet Caleb, next to oldest at twenty-nine. Lillian has been a librarian."

A chuckle bubbled up in Ethan's chest, but he held it in. His brother's eyes widened in disbelief. For his fun-loving, womanizing brother, she'd chosen a librarian? Did their mother want them to divorce?

Next, Mama grabbed a redhead with green eyes by the hand. "Ruby, this is Gideon, who's twenty-seven and the Angel Springs preacher. Ruby's a young widow."

Gideon grinned at her. The girl returned his smile and put her hand in his. Ethan was shocked by how well they seemed to fit together.

That only left the pretty brunette who had more airs about her than a windstorm blowing off the mountains.

Nudging Ethan, his mother took him by the hand as he reluctantly followed her to the stunning hazel-eyed woman with brown hair. "Beth, this is Ethan, my youngest at twenty-two."

For everyone else she had something to say, but nothing for Ethan? Nothing for Beth? The woman was gorgeous, and somehow he got the feeling she was like a duck out of water. Rich, society girl traveled to the country.

Well, this would certainly be interesting.

Caleb ran his fingers through his hair and strode toward Mama. "You can't mean you did this without consulting us. I'm capable of choosing my own wife when the time comes…"

Olivia put her hands on her hips. "That letter wasn't from Jamie Fraser, Jr.?" She took two steps toward Mama. "Mrs. Fraser, you wrote to me pretending to be your son?"

Mama raised her hands to quiet the murmurs of rising complaints. "Everyone, just hear me out. You girls wanted grooms, and these are the four best men in this state, or any other. They each need a wife and to settle down and have a family."

Jamie clasped his mother by the shoulders. "Mama, may I see you in the kitchen?" He glanced at the women who were all watching him with curious gazes. "Excuse us a moment, ladies."

Ethan shook his head, gazing with curiosity at the woman who sat back and quietly watched the others all tripping over themselves to explain why this wasn't going to work. If anyone could get to their mother, it was Jamie.

When they returned, Ethan could tell that Jamie had gotten nowhere. The weddings were still on, but Caleb had apparently overheard their brother's conversation with Mama and was now fighting mad.

"You told Jamie? He knew about this and just happened to forget to tell us?"

"He knew, but I swore him to secrecy. He didn't know I'd included Olivia for him, but he needs a wife the same as the three of you." She tossed up her hands. "Land's sakes, you know Jake and Cat need a mother to tame them."

Jamie was always reminding them he was the oldest. Once again, he'd done something that let them all know he was in charge. He'd gone along with his mother's cockamamie idea, yet Ethan chuckled. This time Jamie's own shenanigans had burned him.

Mama met the angry gaze of each son. "I want you boys to have the same thing your father and I did." Her voice softened. "You have no idea how wonderful it is to have a life partner who shares everything and always supports your ideas."

Boy, she had shoved that knife in and was twisting that handle in order to get her way. Next would come the tears, and slowly, each one of them would crumble and give her what she wanted just so the water works would come to an end.

She pulled a handkerchief from her sleeve and dabbed at her eyes. "We can talk more about this later."

She motioned toward the stairs. "Ladies, if you'd like to freshen up after your ride, go on up. Olivia and Lillian are in the room at the end of the hall on the left. Ruby and Beth are in the second room on the right. The fire has been lit in each room."

Ruby set down her cup and rubbed a handkerchief across her forehead. "I could sure use a few minutes of rest." She turned and climbed the stairs.

Beth hugged her arms as she followed Ruby. Going up the stairs, she turned and glanced back at Ethan, letting her eyes roam over him. "I don't think I'll ever get warm again."

He hoped she got a good look because no matter what her story, he wouldn't be standing in front of a preacher saying any vows anytime soon.

Lillian was the last to leave. She sent Mama a cool glance. "I don't mean to hurt your feelings, ma'am, but you shouldn't have impersonated your sons. That's lying and not fair to anyone concerned."

"I did what I thought was best for my sons," Mama responded in that tone Ethan had learned to recognize long ago that brooked no argument.

With the women gone, all four men began to speak at once. Caleb's voice was loudest, Jamie stood rigid at their mother's side, and Gideon's face was red with rage. Ethan stood back, arms crossed, knowing he wasn't marrying the girl.

Mama left the room then returned, clanging the dinner triangle to get their attention. "Calm down, boys."

Caleb leaned forward toward his mother, his hands on his hips, his eyes flashing fire. "We're not boys any longer, Mama. It's time you realized we're grown men with the right to choose our own wives."

"I know you're men, but you'll always be my boys." She waggled a finger at them. "So don't sass me, Caleb. You worry me most. Don't think you've hidden that you're out carousing until all hours. You're going down a dangerous path, and I aim to see you settle down and raise a family if I have to hogtie you to achieve that goal."

She took a deep breath. "Milly has the table ready for you to sit down like the gentlemen I raised, and we'll talk this through."

Like soldiers called to duty, they marched into the kitchen. Only, Ethan knew he would soon be a deserter.

When they'd all seated themselves, Mama took her place at the head of the table. "Your father and I always believed you four were the best sons anyone ever had. I still believe that, but you haven't honored your promise to marry. Ethan, you're the only one who can skate by on that vow because you're still young. But I see you trying to copy everything Caleb does." Shaking her head, she dabbed a handkerchief to her eyes.

Here came the crying jag. His mother should have been an actress.

Caleb leapt to his feet. "Mama, you're making me sound like the blackest soul in all of Colorado. I do my share of the work same as Jamie and Ethan."

Jamie yanked on his arm. "Sit and listen to what Mama has to say. She isn't through yet."

Mama dabbed her eyes again and sniffed a couple of times while she waited for Caleb to take his seat. "This deep snow means the ladies are stuck here, so we'll have the weddings right away. Milly and I will have everything ready by tomorrow morning."

She stood and waved her handkerchief as she spoke, like she was waving them off to war. "The brides have come here in good faith, and their reputations are at stake. Mine, too, if you don't cooperate. And we can't have single men and single ladies sleeping under the same roof. You four will spend tonight at Caleb's."

Jamie and Gideon glared at Caleb. Ethan smirked; he knew what Caleb had hidden over at his house. He wasn't staying there; he was going home to his loft in the barn.

Shaking his head, Caleb stretched out his long legs and crossed his arms over his chest, staring at the table.

Ignoring the exchange, Mama gestured to the corner. "Milly and I packed you each clean clothes in those satchels. Take them and get out of here until ten o'clock tomorrow morning." She pointed a finger at each of the men. "See that you show up then, or I'll bring Pete with a shotgun. Don't think for a minute I won't."

Ethan frowned. Now that could definitely cause a problem.

He had less than twenty-four hours to convince his mother this marriage was a mistake.

~

After checking her room, Beth gathered in the master bedroom with the other three brides. Gazing around, she noticed the quilt on the bed was a beautiful wedding ring pattern in bright red and blue instead of pastels, but it didn't compare to the rich silks on her coverlet at home.

Near the window, a small lamp table separated a couple of rocking chairs that if she had her way, would soon be on the front porch where they belonged.

The furniture in the room was quaint, but she wouldn't be here long to see to any changes. Once she had a copy of the marriage license, she was on her way back to Chicago as a married woman.

Lillian paced the room with sharp steps. "I've a good mind to leave the minute the snow stops. We were deceived."

Olivia turned to face Lillian. "We're here, so let's wait and see what Mrs. Fraser has to say this evening. I haven't even met Jamie's children yet."

Lying on the bed and looking pale, Ruby waved a limp hand. "Y'all can do what you want. I'm staying and marrying Gideon. He's a good-looking man and has a sweet smile."

Beth hugged her arms. "All four are handsome, and they act respectfully. Ethan's emerald gaze certainly warms a girl and left me breathless. Don't think I'll leave, for now."

Olivia sent her a questioning glance. "What do you mean, *for now*? Once we're wed, you can't change your mind like you would about which hat to wear."

Beth tossed her hair over her shoulder. "Of course you can. Haven't you heard of divorce?"

Lillian gasped. "Divorce? Surely you wouldn't go back on your marriage vows. If you marry Ethan, that will be forever."

"Not every marriage is made in heaven. My parents' certainly wasn't." These women were such country bumpkins who probably thought that ring on their finger promised them happily ever after to go with their patchwork quilts.

Lillian took a step toward her. "But that doesn't mean yours won't—"

"Ladies." Olivia clapped her hands. "This isn't solving our dilemma. If you've glanced out the window, you know we're already buried in snow and more's still falling. We can't leave for who knows how long. If we don't wed, then our reputations will be ruined."

Lillian tapped a finger against her cheek. "Not only that, but I don't have the money to repay Mrs. Fraser for our expenses and the marriage broker's fee."

With that announcement, Beth's stomach tightened. Her trust fund was all wrapped up with a nice bow waiting for her father to hand over to her former fiancé. Currently, she was penniless. "You mean we'd owe them money if we don't go through with the marriage?" Why did everything in life seem to revolve around cash, especially with regard to marriage?

Olivia studied her like she was the stupidest person in the room. "Of course. Didn't you read the contract? If we renege, we have to return the money provided for the fare and meal costs, and repay the broker's fee."

Frowning, Lillian put her hands on her hips. "Surely, you read the document before you committed, Beth."

Refusing to meet their gazes, Beth stared at her hands. These women had no clue what had prompted her to sign up to become a mail-order bride. They had no idea what she'd seen to send her running from a society wedding. And she wasn't going to tell them. "I was in a bit of a hurry, so I just signed. If you remember, I barely made the train."

Olivia sighed, then held out her hand. "I'm staying. Who's with me?"

After a moment's hesitation, the other three brides stacked their hands on Olivia's.

What choice did Beth have? There was no chance to change her mind and return home. Her only option was to stay and marry Ethan Fraser. But that didn't mean this marriage would be forever.

~

Ethan stayed behind when his brothers left for Caleb's house, where the voluptuous Desiree was stashed away. He didn't want to spend the night with his brothers. But then, he didn't want to marry Beth either.

"Ethan, follow your brothers," his mother said, staring at him.

"I'm not staying at Caleb's and I'm not marrying that girl."

His mother's brows drew together in that frown that had gotten to him since he was a young boy. Why was it she had a way of doing things to get him to obey her? And why, at twenty-two, was he still letting her affect him?

"I'll find my own wife," he informed her.

She sighed. "I know you don't like this, but Beth has come all the way from Chicago, thinking there was a man waiting for her. What will happen to her if you don't make her your wife? If you're my son, you'll marry this girl tomorrow."

Fury filled Ethan, and he rose from the table. Not only had her decision affected his life, but if he rejected Beth, his mother would have ruined her reputation as well. That wasn't right. She couldn't play with people's emotions and lives in this manner. It was a dangerous game that eventually would hurt someone.

"You've made your last decision for me. I'll marry this girl because it's not fair for her to have come all this way and not be married, but don't you ever make another decision for me. Are we clear?"

"Ethan," his mother said. "I didn't expect you to take this so hard. Of all my boys, I thought you would be the easiest."

"Well, you thought wrong." He stood. "You've overstepped your rights. I'm a man, and I'm the only one who can make decisions regarding my life."

"Ethan, you know I'm only trying to look out for you."

"You're fooling yourself if you believe that. I think you did this because of your desire to see all your boys married before you took your last breath." Ethan turned and walked out the door, his anger so intense he knew the cold walk to Caleb's would be good for him.

"And stay at Caleb's, so it's known that none of you boys were near the house tonight," his mother yelled out the door at him.

Really? Who was going to know? The ranch hands? The stars? The coyotes?

Trudging through the snow, he just wanted to reach his brother's house and rest. He didn't want to have to listen to his brother go on and on about that sweet little piece he had hidden. That woman was trouble, and she was going to be Caleb's downfall if he wasn't careful.

As he topped the rise, he saw Caleb's small three-room cabin. He dreaded going inside but knew he should. His brothers would be reeling from the blow their mother had just dealt them.

Entering the house, he heard raised voices.

Jamie, spat angrily, "What the hell do you use for a brain? As if things aren't bad enough with four brides arriving, you've got a saloon girl stashed here."

"I didn't know the girls were arriving, did I?" He stabbed a finger against Jamie's chest and leaned into his face. "Because my big brother kept that fact a secret."

Jamie knocked away his hand. "Only because Mama made me promise on my honor. I only found out when I caught her writing a letter. If she hadn't looked so guilty when I walked in, I never would have read part of the page."

Caleb rubbed his hands together. "Well, you three can make yourselves a bed wherever you find a spot. I'm going to my room with Desiree."

Jamie stepped in front of him, stopping him at the door. "No, you're not."

Gideon stood beside Jamie. "This has gone on long enough, Caleb. Not only are you leading a reckless life, but you're also encouraging Ethan to follow you. Starting tonight, you reform, and tomorrow, you marry Lillian, the pretty woman who's waiting to become your wife."

Just because Ethan went to town with Caleb, everyone believed he was doing what his brother was known for. Women and liquor. The ladies were definitely nice, but the alcohol left him feeling bad and wishing he'd stayed home.

So no, he wasn't following in Caleb's footsteps, but he'd given up on trying to convince everyone otherwise. People believed what they wanted, and he was tired of trying to assure them of the truth.

"Hell and damnation." Caleb shook his fist at them. "I deserve one last night before I become a shackled husband. Desiree's waiting for me on the other side of that door. It's taken me months to get her out here."

Jamie smirked. "That's cause she was busy making the rounds of everyone else's beds."

Caleb pulled back his arm to swing at Jamie, but Gideon grabbed his fist to stop him. "I know we're all taken aback by this circumstance, but fighting among ourselves won't solve anything."

Tugging on the cuffs of his shirt, Caleb said, "That Lillian looks like she has a steel rod up her—"

Gideon put his hand over Caleb's mouth. "Don't besmirch any of those women. Each came here with good intentions, thinking one of us had sent for her. If we don't marry them, not only will we ruin their reputations, but we could ruin Mama's standing in the community."

Ethan sat back with crossed arms and let his brothers fight this battle. His mother had him in quite a quandary. If he didn't marry Beth, not only was her reputation ruined, but his mother's as well. And that would make everyone the victim of his mother's scheme. Beth was beautiful, warm, and maybe she was nice, he hadn't even gotten the chance to speak to her, but that didn't mean they should be man and wife.

Caleb batted away Gideon's hand. "Is that right, little brother? Well, she just likes to reign over the other mothers because you're a preacher. Anyway, who'll know if we don't marry those gals?"

Jamie said, "Everyone who saw them leave the train or who knows someone who saw them, which means everyone in Angel Springs and for miles around."

Caleb gave a derisive laugh. "Let me get this straight. You think I'm marrying that stiff-necked spinster and settling her in with Desiree and me? You're crazy."

Gideon met Jamie's gaze. "What about Pete's house? Desiree could stay there, and he could move into the bunkhouse for a few days."

Jamie nodded. "Sounds like a good plan. Pete's a decent guy and will help us out. We can sneak her over there at dawn tomorrow."

The door opened a crack, and Desiree peeked out. "I can hear you, you know. I'm not a chair or a lamp to be shoved around like unwanted furniture."

Gideon bowed slightly. "Begging your pardon, Miss Desiree. We're merely trying to accomplish what's best for you and for the rest of the people on the ranch until the snow lets up and you can go home."

Her generous breasts heaved, drawing the gazes of all four men, and Ethan had to laugh. She was a saloon girl, and his brother was fighting to keep her.

"If you put it that way, I'd appreciate some time off. My feet could use a rest from all that lugging drinks back and forth. But y'all better be ready to calm down Charlie after I don't show up for work for a few days."

Ethan watched Gideon struggle to gaze at her eyes, rather than her chest. "Right. We'll make sure someone explains it all to him."

"Well, all right. Goodnight." She closed the door on the men.

Caleb glared at each of his brothers. "See what you've done? I could be sleeping on a soft mattress with a warm, willing woman. Instead, I'm stuck in here staring at your sorry faces."

His eyes snapped with anger as he waved around the room. "Look, I don't have enough blankets to supply pallets. Unless Mama included bedding in your valises, everybody has to sleep on the hard floor. I'm taking the spot nearest the fireplace. I hope you three freeze your asses off." Instead of lying down, Caleb sat cross-legged on the floor.

For a moment, silence hung over the men as Ethan contemplated his bride. The woman's burnished mahogany hair and hazel eyes made a man's heart pound, but she hardly appeared to have come from a farm or ranch, and he'd bet his best horse she had no idea how to work their outfit.

"I swear I will not marry that Lillian. Guess she's not that bad looking, but I'm not ready to wed. When I am, I can choose my own wife, and she won't be some old dried-up virgin."

Gideon sank onto the floor beside Caleb. "Let's talk, big brother."

Ethan leaned back against the sofa, knowing he wouldn't get any place softer. The image of Beth came to mind. He had a choice, marry the girl or walk away. Her reputation versus his decision to marry. His mother's standing in the community.

Could he be a bad guy and walk away from it all? What should he do?

~

Early the next morning, the women darted around in a frenzy in the master bedroom, as Beth's stomach roiled with fear and uncertainty. Part of her wanted to run out the door into the snow and tell them no, she wasn't marrying that handsome man she didn't know.

Her sensible side was reminding her she'd left everything behind in Chicago. She had no choice but to marry a stranger. All while she was listening to these chattering excited women who thought Santa had arrived and brought them an early Christmas gift, a wedding.

Olivia held up a lavender foulard gown with a white lace collar and shook it. "I should have hung this up last night, so more of the wrinkles would disappear. I wonder if we have time to press our things."

Lillian shook her head in response. "I already asked, but there's too much going on in the kitchen with food preparation. We'll have to make do." She held up a white grosgrain dress decorated with pink embroidery. Smoothing her hand along the skirt, she touched the pink roses and trailing vines and leaves.

Ruby laid her hand over her stomach. "I'll wear my green traveling suit. I brushed it this morning, and I think it looks better than anything else I have."

None of the dresses were high fashion, but they were worthy of a decent wedding. Whereas Beth's own dress was all she had. Never having packed for herself, she'd just grabbed what she'd had to have and left the rest behind. "This is the best thing I have."

Olivia glanced over at Beth and frowned. "Why don't I ask Mrs. Fraser if she has something appropriate?"

Beth chewed her lip for a few seconds. "I-I don't know. I guess you could."

Yes, she knew she was supposed to be a mail-order bride, but when she'd gotten on that train leaving Chicago, she'd never given much thought to the man waiting on this end of the track. It had been a quick fix to a bad situation, mainly, it had been a way out of town.

In a few minutes, Olivia and Mrs. Fraser entered the room and presented Beth with her mother-in-law to-be's own cream silk wedding gown. It was pretty in an antique way. The material had not yellowed, and the dress was beautiful for being over thirty years old. While the dress was a perfect fit, it also made her stop and realize she really was getting married today. Right away. Her heart leaped into her throat. What had she done? In her fear ,she'd left one husband to-be, now it appeared she'd run straight into the arms of a stranger.

She swallowed the panic that clutched at her stomach. "This is lovely. I'll have the best dress there."

Oh dear, she hadn't meant to say what she'd thought. "Uh, no offense meant," she quickly apologized to the other women.

Olivia shook her head and said quietly, "None taken."

Mrs. Fraser glanced nervously at the women. "I need to get back to the kitchen. Ten o'clock will soon arrive, and I still have to change and do my hair."

When she'd gone, Beth twirled to straighten the train, which flowed from the dress. "I could do a whole lot worse. Ethan is handsome, and Mrs. Fraser really is a nice woman." But that didn't mean she was convinced the right thing for her to do was to marry Ethan.

Lillian crossed her arm. "Who'll soon be our mother-in-law, even though she deceived each of us and her sons. I'm not sure how I feel about that. I had no intention of marrying a man dragged to the altar."

Ruby sat on a rocker. "She had her boys' welfare in mind, and we each needed a groom. I don't see a problem as long as the men show up and go through with the wedding."

Beth's eyes widened. "If we're snowed in, who will perform the ceremony?"

"Gideon is a minister. He can officiate," Olivia said.

The clock seemed to rush toward the hour when Beth would have to decide if she should marry a man she didn't know, only to obtain the marriage license. It felt wrong, even if it would solve all her problems. Yet, this man would be waiting, expecting a wedding night, a forever after, and she could only promise him until she could get back to town.

At ten o'clock, Milly rapped on the door. "The men are ready. It's time."

Fear almost strangled Beth, she knew it was time. Time to make a decision.

Dear God, what did she do? Marry him or run yet again?

"Good luck, ladies," Olivia said as they filed out of the room with Beth still no closer to making her mind up about what to do.

Chapter Two

Ethan tried to listen to the words his brother was saying, but all he could do was stare at the woman standing across from him, holding his hands. He could feel her trembling and see the uncertainty reflected in her beautiful hazel eyes.

What was she thinking on their wedding day? Why would a woman travel hundreds of miles to marry a man she'd never met? How could she be certain she was getting a man worthy of marrying her?

Yesterday, he'd been furious with his mother finding him a woman when he'd been flirting with that cute little girl in town. Alyssa knew what to expect living on a ranch in the mountains.

Last night, he'd learned that Beth was from Chicago—a city girl. The clothing she'd arrived in was stylish and made from expensive cloth. He doubted she was used to the rigors of ranch life away from civilization. She gave off high society airs, and his family were certainly not rich socialites, even for the town of Angel Springs.

He'd thought long and hard about whether or not he was going to marry this woman. Part of him wanted to defy his mother, but the other part, the manly part, was asking him if he'd lost his mind.

Look at the girl. She was prettier than the mountains in springtime. And her figure was exactly what a man dreamed of holding in his arms—rounded in all the right places, as tempting as apple pie. From what he'd seen yesterday, her spirit seemed strong. He couldn't abide a weak kneed woman who demanded attention.

So far, most of the girls he'd met were giggly, fainting, spineless dolls without brains. He wanted a partner. A wife and mother to his children. A woman who would love him for the man he was and who would make him strive to be even better.

"Do you take this woman to be your wife?" his older brother, the reverend, asked him.

This was his last opportunity to bow out. He stared at the woman touching him, promising him forever. There was something in her eyes that called to him, made him want to comfort, protect, and bed her all at the same time.

"I do," he said, knowing this commitment was for a lifetime. That he'd just bound himself to a woman he didn't know. But Beth was intriguing. She was beautiful. She carried herself like a woman of importance, yet she'd arrived with just the clothes on her back and a small valise. Nothing else. She was wearing his mother's wedding dress, which filled him with pride, but also made him curious. Why hadn't she brought more clothes?

"Do you, Beth Worthington, take this man to be your husband?" Gideon asked.

"I do," she responded, her hands quivering in his. Her big hazel eyes, simmering with a gold tone that tantalized him, gazed at him with apprehension.

With a sudden realization, he knew she was just as scared as him.

No matter what reason brought her to Colorado, he wanted to learn more about her and her family. Where were her mother and father?

"By the power invested in me, I now pronounce all of us man and wife. You may kiss your brides."

Ethan stared at the woman he'd just married. For a moment, their life together flashed before his eyes and he swallowed.

Their journey together started right now. Tonight was their wedding night. This moment was their first kiss. Pulling her into his arms, he kissed her full mouth, feeling the texture of her soft lips, wanting the memory of their wedding to be a lasting one. His hands cupped her face as he angled her head for a deeper exploration before he released her mouth. Slowly, he opened his eyes.

Stunned, she returned his gaze like she didn't know what to think.

Smiling, he let go of her and stepped back, instantly missing the connection of her body with his.

Her fingertips reached up and touched her mouth in surprise. Obviously, she'd felt the connection just as he had.

He smiled at her. "Mrs. Fraser, I'll do my best to make you a good husband." And he meant the words, even if he didn't know his wife.

"Oh my. We're married," she whispered. "This isn't a dream."

He chuckled. "Nope. You're here in Angel Springs, Colorado, and now you're Beth Fraser, my wife."

She seemed to be in shock, and he wondered why. Wasn't this what she'd traveled all that way for? What had she expected?

At least she'd had the advantage of knowing she was getting married ahead of time.

Since yesterday, he'd refused to speak to his mother. She knew he was angry, but what she didn't know was this had been her last opportunity to tell him what to do. He was a man, and a man made decisions on his own, not because his mother told him to. Next time, his answer to her would be *no*.

"I'll help you move your things out to the barn later today."

The brothers had all stayed together last night to appease their mother and to commiserate together, but tonight, he planned on returning to his own bed.

"Barn?"

"Yes, I live in the loft above the stables."

"With the animals?" Her eyes widened in alarm, and he could see she was appalled at the idea of where they would be living…at least until he built them a house.

He smiled. "They don't usually come up to the loft."

"But what about the smells?"

He shrugged. "You get used to it."

Her hazel eyes widened, and he could see the horror reflected in her gaze. If she was one of those women who complained about every little thing to do with living in the barn, there could be trouble. He had every intention of building them a house, but not until winter was over. And besides, it was something he'd always planned on doing with his wife—designing the house plans then building the structure.

"Can't we live here in the house?"

There was no way he was going to begin their marriage in the same house as his mother, under her scrutiny. He'd watched Jamie go through that with his first wife, and he liked having his own space. "No room. Besides, we need our own place. You'll get used to it."

~

Later that evening after the men had done their chores and returned for supper, Beth watched the other women with their new husbands. She'd never dreamed it would be this awkward. She'd never given much thought to the wedding night. And now, here she was married to a man she didn't know, moving out to live in the barn.

Elizabeth Worthington, of the Chicago Worthingtons, debutante, would be living in a loft above farm animals. Wouldn't the girls be laughing at how far she'd come down in the world?

One minute she'd been engaged to one of the wealthiest men in Chicago, and the next moment, she'd been running to escape a wedding. But instead, she'd run from one wedding to another, and in the process, she'd lost her social status.

Sure, she could write a letter to her father, and she knew he would "fix" this latest scrape she'd gotten into, but he'd also want her to marry Henry Frank Thurston III.

She shuddered at the thought and pushed away the memory that had sent her running in the middle of the night.

Holding onto Ethan's arm, she walked with him into the dining room, where Milly was laying out food.

"All the couples should sit together," her new mother-in-law called to them.

"Let the wedding feast begin," her husband said beneath his breath, his tone sarcastic.

He sounded almost angry, and she suddenly wondered, had he wanted this wedding? She'd seen the surprised look on his face yesterday when the women had arrived, but somehow she'd thought he'd yearned to get married.

What if he didn't desire her any more than she fancied him?

This was not a wedding feast. Beth had attended parties that were far more elegant than this. She'd expected to come down in life, but she'd never dreamed how far, nor how much she'd be forced to give up, to live the type of life she wanted. But this wouldn't last forever because just as soon as the snow melted and she could get to town, she had every intention of finding her way back to Chicago. She was married. No one could force her into a loveless marriage with an old man.

"Green beans?" Ethan asked, holding out a dish, his earthy brown eyes twinkling with a sparkle she feared. The man was in for quite a disappointment. She was only here temporarily.

Now, she could go back to her father and say, "Sorry, I'm married," but she couldn't tell him why she'd gotten cold feet, and she had to give the scandal time to fade.

Quickly, she pushed the thoughts out of her head, concentrating on getting through the wedding feast. They were certainly backward in this part of the world.

Glancing down the table at her new temporary family, she felt lucky. Of the Fraser men, she'd married the youngest and the best looking. Though peering at Ethan's oldest brother, she knew how Ethan would look in ten years. The resemblance between the brothers was uncanny, and ten years separated Jamie and Ethan. But she wouldn't be here to see that transformation. She'd be back in Chicago where she belonged. Back in society with servants to take care of her every need.

"So, why don't each of my new daughters-in-law tell us a little bit about yourselves?" Mrs. Fraser nodded at Olivia to begin the inquisition.

Beth listened to each girl tell her story and wondered about these women. Why would you traipse so far from civilization if you had a choice? What was the real reason these women were snowbound in the mountains of Colorado with this family?

When it came her turn, Beth knew she could never tell them the truth. There was no way she would explain why she'd become a mail-order bride. Never.

Taking a deep breath, she smiled and let the lies flow. "My mother died when I was ten, during the great fire of 1871 in Chicago. She'd gone to visit my grandmother and became trapped, unable to get home."

A sigh was heard around the table. That much was at least true.

"Such a tragic fire," Mrs. Fraser said.

"Soon after that, Father sent me off to The Refined Arts School for Young Ladies. When I graduated, there were no suitors in sight, so I decided to take matters into my own hands. I signed up as a mail-order bride, and here I am."

What she refused to say was how after she debuted, she'd agreed to marry Henry Frank Thurston III, one of the richest men in Chicago. Or what she'd learned two nights before they were to marry had sent her running out of town as fast as she could go. But these people didn't need to know everything about her past. In fact, the less the better.

"You poor dear," her new mother-in-law said. "Well, we're glad you're here with us now."

"Thank you, Ma'am," Beth said and glanced over at her husband who hadn't said a word but who stared at her, his dark brows raised. For some reason, she knew he didn't believe her.

The man was absolutely gorgeous, and there was something so compelling about his eyes. They warmed her and sent chills trickling down her spine like she'd never felt before. And that kiss at the ceremony had been downright scandalous and wonderful.

Sure, she'd been kissed before, but Ethan's lips had left her warmer than a blanket on a cold winter night. The man knew how to use his mouth for things other than talking, but he was in for a shocker when she told him there would be no consummation on their wedding night. She wasn't about to share a bed with a man she barely knew. But she'd used him for what she needed. When the snow storm ended and she had the marriage license in hand, then she would return to Chicago. Hopefully by the time she got back, the scandal of her called-off wedding would have been replaced by some new egregious act.

Gideon rose and helped his wife from her chair. "I believe I'll escort Ruby into the parlor."

Chairs scraped back as the men took their brother's cue and helped their new wives rise from the dinner table. Beth felt Ethan's hand touch her elbow, and a zip of warmth zinged along her spine, like a good hot toddy.

Soon, they were all seated in front of the blazing fire in the parlor.

"Let me show you your new home," Ethan said quietly, his voice low and warm.

Taking a deep breath, she gazed at his mother, not wanting to leave this sanctity. "I think we should stay."

"For what?"

"Cake?"

He laughed. "Come on. Milly didn't bake a cake."

"Oh," she said, disappointed. She wasn't ready to retire for the evening. She wasn't ready to face him in their home. She wasn't about to let him convince her they were married and should consummate their vows.

Swallowing the fear she could feel bubbling up inside her, she glanced around the room. Lillian and Caleb had already left, and that just left Ruby and Olivia with their new husbands, and Mama Fraser.

Beth's lungs tightened, and for a moment, she couldn't breathe. What had she done? She'd gone from Prairie Avenue, the richest street in Chicago, to living above nasty, stinky farm animals in the loft of the barn.

Maybe she should have stayed and married Henry. He never would have bothered her.

~

The light was quickly fading, yet snow continued to fall. A shiver rippled through Beth as they hurried toward the barn, snowflakes peppering them.

Ethan wrapped his arm around her and brought her in close. "Are you cold?"

What could she say? She was freezing from the frigid temperatures, but she feared his touch. She might be his wife, but they would not be sleeping in the same bed tonight. "I'm okay. Maybe you could show me around the ranch."

He laughed. "In the snow? It's cold. We're having a blizzard. Ask me again when the sun is shining."

Right now, she didn't care, as long as it kept them out of that barn and away from the confrontation she knew was coming.

The very idea of consummating their marriage had her quivering like a lion at the North Pole. She gazed at him as they walked along a path to the barn. "Why did we leave the party?"

"I thought it might be good to get to know you a little better," he said, his head tilted away to keep the snow from hitting him in the face.

Ice was flowing through her veins, but Beth slowed her feet. She wasn't looking forward to the first contest of wills with her new husband, about how they would be sleeping in separate beds and the list of demands she intended to give him. After all, as his wife, she expected to be treated well. All she needed were some new clothes, a maid, and a one-way ticket back to Chicago. She'd reimburse him just as soon as she returned home. Her father could send him a check.

"Let's hurry and get out of this wet cold. The snow is coming down hard."

Back home, they had their share of wintry weather. She was use to frigid temperatures; her tremors were more anticipatory than from actual chills. "We have lots of snow in Chicago."

"But you don't have mountains."

"No, we don't have mountains, but a man or woman can get lost in a snowstorm and freeze to death in no time."

They reached the barn, and she hesitated when he opened the door. Inside would be stinky animals. She wasn't a big fan of cows and pigs.

"Come on," he encouraged. "It's not bad. I've done some work on the loft. I think you'll like it."

She raised her brows at him. Obviously, the man had no idea of where she'd lived because there was no way a barn could be a decent home. Taking a deep breath of fresh air, she stepped inside, expecting the worst odors. Holding the air trapped in her lungs, she noticed the animals were all in stalls and seemed to gaze at her oddly. Finally forced to gasp for air, she realized the smells were of hay and feed.

A big dog came running to Ethan, and she stepped behind him, afraid of the animal.

"Hi, Lady, meet your new mistress. She'll be living with us now."

Beth stared at Ethan. "You have a dog?"

Scratching the animal behind her ears, he said, "Yes. I've had her since she was a pup."

When he was gone, the dog would not be in their house. Oh, but wait…they didn't have a house. They had a *barn*.

"Dogs are nasty. They have fleas." When she was a child, she'd asked for a dog, but her mother had refused to let her have a puppy, telling her only lower class people spent money on pets. She'd never asked again.

"Lady, did you hear that? Your new mistress thinks you have fleas." He continued to rub the dog, and she gazed up at him with adoration. "Have you ever had a dog?"

"No, my mother didn't approve," she said, watching the animal who only had eyes for Ethan.

He took her hand and laid it on the animal's soft fur. The big shaggy mutt turned kind brown eyes at her, clearly inviting Beth to touch her. The dog licked Beth's hand. Warmth flooded through her as she stared at the large animal, shocked by the acceptance.

"Oh my," she said with a laugh. "I think she likes me."

"Lady loves everyone," he said, patting the dog on the head. "Come on, let's get you upstairs."

Walking past a tack room and what looked like a woodworking room, they traveled down a short hall that had a staircase at the end. While most barns just had a ladder up to the loft, this one had actual stairs at the back of the building.

Beth sighed with relief. The idea of crawling up a ladder in her long skirts every day was not appealing in the least. "Stairs," she said with a smile.

"I told you this barn doesn't have the typical loft. It's going to be okay for a while. Later, I'll build us a house. But for now, this will do."

Why was she reacting? It didn't really matter because she would be long gone before the home was ever built.

Taking her elbow, Ethan led her up the stairs to a door at the top. Turning the knob, he swung her up into his arms.

Gazing up into his soft earthy eyes, she felt like her heart would beat out of her chest as she stared at him. "What are you doing?"

"I'm carrying you over the threshold," he replied. "Isn't that what a husband is supposed to do?"

She giggled, surprised by her reaction, as relief and excitement flooded her body all at once. "I forgot."

After entering the room, he set her down and watched as she glanced around the open room.

The largest object in the center of the room was the bed. Sitting snug against the wall and covered with a beautiful quilt, that object of fear drew her gaze immediately.

Shelves lined with books graced the walls around the main living area, and a large black potbelly stove resided in the corner. Two wooden chairs and a small sofa sat close to the fire. A small kitchen was in one corner with a sink. In a far corner was a claw foot tub with a screen sitting beside it.

Overall, it wasn't a bad living space, compact and small, but it had character. It wasn't what she expected to find when she thought of Ethan.

"Mom sent over the screen earlier today. She said you might like getting undressed behind there and enjoy your bath more."

Beth nodded. "She's right."

The very idea of disrobing with Ethan around was nerve wracking. She walked around the room, gazing at the bookshelves. Turning to him, she asked, "Do you like to read?"

"Very much. I enjoy I.M. Lyon's books."

"Oh, I've never heard of that author."

"He's one of those dime novel, Western writers. You're welcome to borrow a copy."

"Thanks," she said, thinking if she could keep him reading, then he wouldn't be interested in having marital relations with her.

Suddenly, she came upon the bed. Her throat constricted, and she glanced at him. "There's only one bed."

"Yes, that's all I need up here."

"But where will you sleep?"

He laughed. "Right beside you."

She shook her head. They could not share the same bed. That was a sure road to disaster. "Oh, no. You'll have to sleep on the floor."

He walked to her, gazed down into her eyes, and quietly said, "We're married. We're husband and wife. We can sleep together."

The man was handsome, rugged; his arms were muscled and strong, and no, she wasn't sharing that bed with him. Not now. Not ever, but he didn't have to know that just yet.

"No, my parents were married, and they didn't even share the same room. I'm not sleeping in the same bed with you."

"My parents slept together the forty years they were married. And I'm not sleeping on the floor. It's too cold and I work too hard, not to get enough rest. If you want to wait a while for us to consummate our marriage, I understand. I'll give you some time, but we're going to be in that bed together."

Beth placed her hands on her hips. "No, we're not."

A frown creased his forehead. She could see he wasn't happy, but he wasn't going to argue with her any longer. So maybe he'd just give up and walk away, letting her have the bed.

"Then Mrs. Fraser, you may take the sofa or the floor. Your choice. Lady usually sleeps on the rug by the fire, but I'm sure she would share the space with you."

Beth stared open-mouthed at Ethan, who calmly moved to a chest and began to remove his clothes. Her new husband was a stubborn, irritating man who was refusing to give in to her demands.

Chapter Three

Early the next morning, Ethan rose and began to dress. His lovely wife lay on the sofa, a blanket pulled up to her neck. It had taken her almost an hour last night to get ready for bed, and then she'd told him to turn out the lamp before she'd crawled under the covers on the sofa. She'd refused to share his bed and that frustrated him. After all, for a man like himself, what was he getting out of this marriage so far? He was married to a woman he didn't know and so far, he wasn't getting to share the marital bed.

Yet, in so many ways, he understood she required some time. Maybe they both needed the chance to get to know one another before they became a real married couple. He knew very little about her family, her previous life, or the reason she'd become a mail-order bride. All he knew was he was forever tied to this gorgeous woman who was used to a more comfortable way of life.

Turning up the lantern in the loft, he gazed at her. She was curled up in a ball, sound asleep on the sofa. Gently, he pulled the blanket away from her face and pressed his lips to her forehead. He trailed his kisses down her cheek until he reached her mouth. Softly, he moved his lips over hers.

He'd been thinking about the way her lips had felt since that kiss at the ceremony yesterday afternoon, the way she'd tasted, and how her body had fit within his arms. He could only imagine how soft her skin would be against his own.

As his lips covered her mouth, she bolted straight up to a sitting position. "What are you doing?"

"I'm kissing my wife good morning."

"Oh. Good morning." She rubbed her eyes. "It's still dark outside."

He laughed. "Ranch work starts early. Get dressed and we'll meet the others for breakfast at the bunkhouse."

"I think I'll just sleep in."

"Sweetheart, everyone works around the ranch. As my mother likes to say, idle hands are the devil's tool. Come on, get up, and let's get the day started."

Good grief, his mother and the other women's tongues would flay the skin off his wife, if she didn't show up to help them with the ranch chores. No one laid up, unless he was sick or near to dying.

Ethan watched as Beth buried herself beneath the covers.

"You need to hire some servants," she said.

Laughter bubbled up through Ethan. "We have helpers, not servants. They help us take care of the ranch, and we pay them. But there is still plenty of work for everyone. Even you, princess."

Glaring at him over the top of her covers, she rose to a sitting position. "I may have lived like a princess, but I'm not one, so don't call me that name. Now if you will move, I'll get dressed."

He tried not to smile, but he couldn't resist. He was quickly learning his wife had not come from a poor family and was rather spoiled when it came to life. Unfortunately, she was going to have to learn that here on the ranch, everyone pulled his weight. They had no time to indulge socialite women who thought they were too good to get their hands dirty.

He backed away from the sofa. As she stood, she kept the blanket tightly wrapped around her then strolled like a queen behind the screen, glaring at the dog when she passed Lady curled up on the rug in front of the stove.

"I saw your nightgown," he called after her, just to rile her. He had this nasty little streak in him that wanted to make her laugh at herself. So far, she wasn't laughing.

"I'm not wearing a gown," she said, ignoring him and going behind the screen.

For a moment, he was stunned. Then he remembered all she'd brought with her was a small valise. She had no other clothes. She'd brought nothing. Most women traveled with a trunk, yet his snooty wife had left home with only the clothes on her back.

Why would a woman leave without a bag, a chest, or a few treasured belongings? The obvious reason was she'd left in a hurry. But why? The next few days were going to be mighty interesting as he got to know this woman.

The woman moved slower than melting snow in springtime. They should already be on their way, and she wasn't even dressed.

He sank down on the sofa and pulled out his pocket watch. They were late. "Honey, are you almost ready?"

What could she be doing behind that screen? It didn't take that long to put on clothes, did it? He knew women wore more undergarments than men, but still, they were late for breakfast. There might be nothing left by the time they got down to the bunkhouse.

"I'm doing my hair."

"Your hair is beautiful. Let's go."

She came out and laid a metal barrel on top of the stove. "I'm just using the heating iron on my hair. Then I'll be ready."

"Can't you do that after breakfast?"

"No. No one sees me without my hair curled."

If it wasn't their first breakfast as a married couple and if she'd known the way to the bunkhouse, he would have gone off without her. But she had no idea where the building was and he didn't want her to walk in alone. As it was, they would probably suffer a lot of ribbing because they were so late.

And everyone would assume it was because they'd been mating like two animals long into the night and maybe even this morning, when they hadn't even slept in the same bed.

Maybe she could just cook, and he could make coffee. "Do you know how to make eggs? I was thinking maybe we could have breakfast just the two of us here in the loft."

She had the hair iron in her hand, her hair twisted around the barrel. "I've never cooked anything in my life. So no, I don't know how to fix eggs."

So far, this marriage was exactly what he'd been afraid of. Now he was hogtied to a woman who expected him to hire servants, who slept late, who didn't know how to cook, and who refused to share his bed. What was he getting from this union?

Finally, she whirled around, her hair all neatly curled. "Now, I'm ready."

He pulled his pocket watch out and glanced at the time. It had taken her almost an hour to get ready to walk down to breakfast. "Let's go see if there's any food left. We may be going hungry until lunch."

Picking up her shawl, she strolled toward the door. "Tomorrow morning maybe you should go without me."

There was no way he was going to let a wife of his sleep in, while the rest of the ranch worked. It wouldn't be fair to the others, and Ethan was a fair yet stubborn man. Besides, his mother would come searching for Beth, and he wasn't ready to confront his mother for Beth's sake.

"Tomorrow morning, you're going to have chores that need to be done. No one sleeps in at the ranch."

"We'll see about that. Refined ladies do not arise until at least eight o'clock."

Shaking his head, he wondered again what had made this woman decide to become a mail-order bride.

Obviously, it wasn't his status in this world. So why had she chosen him?

"Honey, what the hell made you think you belonged in Colorado?"

~

Beth glanced around at the women who were cleaning up the breakfast dishes, as Mrs. Fraser came toward her and Ethan.

"There you two are. I was beginning to worry. You've missed breakfast. I think there's some coffee left, but everything else is gone. Ethan, the men have already left to check on the cattle."

Ethan didn't acknowledge his mother but instead turned to Beth. "Mom will tell you what your chores are around the ranch. I'll see you at supper tonight." Awkwardly, he reached down and pecked her on the lips then hurried out to join the other men.

Mrs. Fraser shook her head as she watched Ethan go out the door. "He is so much like his brother Caleb, headstrong and stubborn as the day is long. He's really angry with me for bringing you here. But he'll soon get over it, and someday he'll even thank me for finding him a great wife."

A sinking sensation landed like a rock in Beth's stomach. No, Ethan would be even angrier at his mother for sticking him with a wife who'd left him. For there was no way Beth was staying in this godforsaken country. At least in Chicago they cleared the streets of snow, so a woman could walk without dragging her skirt through the muck. Here, the bottom of her skirt was already wet from the snow and mud.

"I have your wedding dress over at Ethan's. I'll return it to you."

"That's fine, dear. The other girls are busy tidying up and helping out. Normally, we eat breakfast and lunch in the bunkhouse and then supper for the family is in the main house every night. You and Ethan may choose to dine with the family at night or in the loft."

"What's a bunkhouse?"

Mrs. Fraser tilted her head and gazed at her then said with a chuckle. "That's where our men live and eat."

"Thanks," Beth said thinking she really didn't want to spend every evening with Mrs. Fraser and at least this way she'd have a choice as to where they could eat, if she didn't like what one place was serving.

"What would you like to do to assist around the home?"

Beth gazed at her with surprise. Ethan had been serious this morning. They really expected her to work around the home? "Normally, I work on my needlepoint, write letters, have lunch with my friends, shop, and approve the menu for cook. Oh, and occasionally, I visit the orphanage and deliver clothing our church has collected for them. I'm great at organizing parties."

The woman stared at her open-mouthed. "What about cleaning and cooking?"

"Oh, the servants take care of running the house."

Mrs. Fraser laughed and wrapped her arm around Beth's shoulders. "Honey, life is not like that on a ranch. Everyone works. Everyone has responsibilities to keep the place running."

"Why not hire servants?"

"We don't need servants. Clara and Patience are our helpers, along with the hired hands, but we do the rest ourselves. Today is laundry day. Why don't you help me and Clara with the laundry? Have you ever washed your own clothes before?"

Beth stared at the woman. "No, never."

What had she gotten herself into? At the time, being a mail-order bride had seemed like a great solution. No one could force her to marry a man who repulsed her. She'd disappear to the West for a couple of months until everything blew over. Then she'd return to her hometown, where she could take up her place in society once again.

Obviously, she'd not thought things through very well. For one thing, her lack of wardrobe was appalling. How could she have left without thinking of her clothing? But then again, her personal maid had always laid out the day's outfit.

God, she missed Maria and how she'd taken such excellent care of Beth. When she got home, she would make certain Maria was given a raise.

Mrs. Fraser shook her head. "Did your mother never do laundry?"

"No, ma'am. We had servants."

"Oh…" She glanced at Beth, and from the expression in Mrs. Fraser's face, Beth knew she'd just been found lacking.

"My maid, Maria, took care of everything for me," she added.

"Well, Maria's not here, so I'll just have to show you. You'll be doing the household laundry to start off with. Plus, every morning, you'll collect the eggs and bring them to the cook. Since you're not used to housekeeping, I'll have Clara show you how we take care of the main house. I know eventually you and Ethan will have your own home. In the spring, we grow a big garden. You'll have your section to tend to."

If the snow wasn't so deep and still coming down, Beth would run back to Chicago immediately. She'd never had to even so much as dust the furniture. She'd depended on servants her whole life. Spending her free time learning to dust and mop a home was not exactly what she'd thought she would be doing on this trip. Then again, she'd watched her servants cleaning house, so how hard could it be?

"Oh, and do you cook?" Mrs. Fraser frowned. "Sorry, I guess that was a silly question, considering you've been taken care of your whole life." She continued. "You might want to spend some time with Milly, our ranch cook. You and Ethan are welcome to eat with all of us at the bunkhouse, but I think there might come a time when the two of you may want to dine alone. It might be nice to fix my son a good meal when he comes in tired from working all day."

Beth had never really considered a life without servants before, and now, she was thinking she would never take them for granted again.

"Oh, one last thing. All of us know how to milk the cows because you just never know when you're going to have to take over that chore from someone else."

Beth's eyes widened. "You touch a cow's tit?"

Her mother-in-law laughed. "It's a teat, dear, and they're used to it. It's really quite simple."

Fear rippled through Beth, and she wanted to cry. This was not what she'd signed up for. She'd agreed to become Ethan's wife, not his servant, and she'd never even considered what his life was like. She'd been told they lived on a sizable ranch, and she'd just assumed they were wealthy and had servants. She never considered she'd be the one working the ranch.

"Let's get busy. The day is already slipping away from us, and soon the men will be coming in from the cold, expecting lunch." Mrs. Fraser hurried off, and Beth just stood there for a moment.

God, what had she gotten herself into? She'd thought the wedding night would be the hardest part, but this was just ridiculous.

~

Snow gently fell, as the blizzard finally sputtered to an end. They would still be snowbound for a few days, but at least the end appeared on the white horizon. Soon, winter would hold them captive, and they would be snug as a bear in a cave until mid-March. But how would his city-bred wife deal with seeing the same people every day? With knowing she couldn't travel past the ranch boundaries for fear of causing an avalanche?

Ethan tossed the bale of hay off the wagon for his brothers to break up with a pitchfork for the cattle.

Gideon hummed a tune beneath his breath. He genuinely seemed cheerful this morning.

"What are you so happy about?" Jamie asked.

"Slept really well last night," he said with a smile.

"That's what usually happens when a man has relations with his wife," Caleb said frowning.

"Come on, guys. It was our wedding night. You know, new beginnings, companionship, eventually love and sex, lots of good ole fashioned marital loving. I kind of like being married," Gideon said.

The men all stopped what they were doing and stared at their brother. Ethan tossed another bale of hay off the wagon, and it almost hit Gideon. "I'm a man. I don't need my mother making decisions for me. She had no right to find me a wife."

"And would you have found someone in town or just continued to follow Caleb around, picking up every skirt you two chased?" Gideon asked.

Ethan glared at Gideon, outrage flowing through his veins. Why did they all believe he was nothing but Caleb's lackey? "There was someone in town I was talking to. The next time I was in Angel Springs, I'd planned on asking her out to dinner. We've been smiling and making eyes at each other for months. I just hadn't acted on the attraction yet."

"There's the problem. You waited too long, and now you're married."

"You could have told Mama no," Jamie said. "We all could have told her no."

Ethan tossed another bale of hay out of the wagon. The chaff flew in all directions, right at the feet of Jamie.

"Yes, I saw how well that worked for you," Ethan said to his oldest brother. "Besides, would that have been fair to Beth? She came all this way."

"I may not have wanted to get married, but it was kind of nice waking up in bed together this morning," Jamie said. "There's nothing like curling around a woman for body heat."

"Yes," Ethan lied, thinking how empty his bed had been last night, knowing there was a woman in the room with him. They were legally married, but she'd refused to sleep in the same bed.

"Little brother, you don't seem to be all that keen on marriage. Did you have a rough wedding night?" Gideon asked, smiling at him.

There was no way he was going to let his brothers know his wedding night had been spent alone. "It was wonderful," he lied. "I'm surprised the noise we were making didn't keep you up last night. What about you, Caleb? You're awfully quiet. Did Lillian find out about Desiree?"

"No. So far I've been able to keep her hidden from Mother and Lillian. This is the last time my mother is going to interfere in my life."

"Agreed," Ethan said.

"Back in biblical times, the parents always found their children's spouses. I feel pretty lucky," Gideon said, tossing hay out to the cattle that were mooing loudly and moving closer to the feed.

Ethan threw another bale down off the wagon. "I have to admit my wife is one hell of a looker."

"Mine ain't so bad herself," Jamie said.

"Mine's prettier than I am," Caleb said.

Ethan wanted to disagree with him but bit back his retort. "Hell, anyone is prettier than you are."

"My wife is lovely," Gideon said. He paused for a moment then turned serious. "This is going to be great. We're all married. Soon our children will be running around the ranch. God had a course of action, and Mother just followed his plan."

"No, I think Mother created the plan and God okayed it," Ethan said. "After all, she went behind our backs and sent for mail-order brides for us. She could've waited and let us make our own decision. She had to jump into our business and give it her touch. Isn't that what she's always done?"

"Maybe. But stop and think about it. If your children don't get married, what are you going to do?" Gideon asked.

Ethan shook his head. "I'm going to tell them there is a great big world out there. Be careful, write often, and don't come back until you're ready to settle down."

"Said like a man who doesn't have children," Jamie responded.

The horse shimmied unexpectedly, and Ethan had to steady himself. They were almost done feeding the stock.

"Yet, here you are. Why hadn't you taken off if you felt that way?" Gideon asked.

"I just wanted to taste the flowers in the neighborhood before I settled on one variety. I'd narrowed it down and was about to start seriously pursuing the garden when low and behold arrives a bride my mother chooses for me,"

Ethan said, thinking of how everything about his marriage was starting off wrong.

He was attracted to Beth, but they were so different. And he still wondered why a girl like her would choose to become a mail-order bride.

Either the men in Chicago were blind or there was a trait he'd yet to see in his wife.

The wind swept across the valley blowing snow and causing Ethan to shiver with cold. He only hoped Beth could find a way to fit into his ranch life. Already she'd been complaining about living above animals and needing servants. Maybe residing in the barn wasn't the best place for them, and come spring, he should see about building them a house.

"Quit complaining. It's done. You're married. You're going to have as much sex as you want, when you want it. Be happy," Jamie said.

"Are you happy?" Ethan asked.

"Deliriously."

"And you, Caleb?"

"Never been better," he responded.

"And Gideon?"

"Wonderful," he said. "What about you? Did you have a good night?"

"The best," he lied. He was not about to admit to his brothers that his stubborn, beautiful wife had slept on the sofa while he'd occupied the bed. Why was he the only one having trouble with his marriage?

Chapter Four

Later that afternoon, Ethan searched all through the house, the barn, everywhere but the loft, looking for Beth. He knew she was not accustomed to working, but he'd hoped he would find her with the other women doing some mundane chore his mother had given them. Finally, he climbed the stairs to the loft, thinking maybe she was settling in.

When he opened the door, he saw her curled up in their bed, her eyes closed, and he realized she was napping. The urge to slip his dirty clothes off and join her in that bed was overwhelming, but he had work to do before he could stop for the day.

Still, he couldn't resist kissing her. Maybe tonight she'd join him, and he could finally claim his wife as his own.

Leaning over the bed, he pressed his mouth to hers and reveled in the softness of her lips. He wanted to continue the exploration, as she moaned and lifted her hand to touch his face. Her eyes opened dreamily, and he smiled at her.

"You're kissing me again."

"I like kissing my wife," he said.

A blush spread across her face, and she quickly sat up in bed. "I guess I got tired. Your mother had me doing laundry this morning. Afterwards, we hung the wet clothes in the kitchen to dry. Then I watched Milly make a pie. She's going to teach me how to cook. Afterward, I helped Olivia with the children. Those two are a handful."

He sank down onto the bed beside her, basically trapping her. He stared into her beautiful hazel eyes and watched her nervously lick her lips. "How long have you been resting?"

"Not long. Your mother told me I should help with the dinner tonight. Is this what life is like here every day? Servitude from sunup to sundown?"

"There's a lot of work involved in keeping a ranch running."

"Don't you ever rest?"

He smiled. "Of course we do, but the animals have to be cared for every day. Then in the spring, it's calving season. A fence needs to be mended. There is always plenty of things that need to be done."

"Speaking of, your mother wants to show me how to milk a cow. Since we live in the barn, she said it might be easiest for me to milk the cows instead of Clara or in case she's busy. I don't want to put my hands on a cow's parts."

Ethan threw back his head and laughed. "It's teats, and it's not that bad. Once you get the hang of squeezing the teats, it'll take very little time."

"But it's an animal," she said with a shudder.

Unable to stop himself, he reached out and brushed a lock of her dark hair away from her face. She was so young, so vulnerable, and so damn tempting he just wanted to strip off his clothes and slide between the sheets with her, but he knew that wouldn't be good.

"Come on," he said rising. He had to get her out of that bed or find himself not being a gentleman and crawling in beside her. When they made love, he wanted for them both to enjoy the experience, not endure it out of duty.

Pulling her boots on, she asked, "Where are we going?"

"I'm going to show you how easy it is to milk the cow." Taking her hand, he pulled her up.

"Wait, let me make certain my hair is still curled."

He laughed and pulled her toward the door. "The cow is not going to care whether your hair is curled or not. It looks gorgeous. Every time you wear it up like that, it's so tempting for me to take the pins out and run my hands through your loose curls. I like your hair."

"Thank you," she said, staring at him while a soft blush spread across her face.

"Come on. I'm going to turn you into a milk maid yet."

"Don't count on it. It's hard to take the city out of the girl."

Lady followed them down the stairs, never far from her master's side when he was in the barn. When they reached the ground floor, he opened the main door of the barn, and a cold blast of wind sent snow swirling. He retrieved a cow from the animal pen and pulled her into the stall.

"Before you do anything, make certain the heifer is tied to a railing. Then I like to give her some feed, as it makes it a nice treat while I'm milking her." He threw the rope around her neck and tied it to a wooden plank then looked back at Beth. She was staring at him, her hazel eyes wide, while she bit her bottom lip.

"You really expect me to do this?"

"Yes, Beth. It's not hard."

"That's easy for you to say since you grew up on a ranch."

"You're right. I did. But anyone can learn."

She crossed her arms over her chest "Ethan, I—"

"I'm going to help you, until you get the hang of it." He took a bucket off the wall and filled it with water. Then he picked up a rag and a bar of soap. "You need to always wash the cow's teats before you began to milk. This cleans off any dirt and manure."

"Manure?" she exclaimed. "I'm *not* milking a cow."

Grinning at her, he pretended to ignore her tantrum. "Yes, Beth. The cow sometimes walks through manure or gets it on her tail. You don't want it in your milk."

"Don't worry. I won't be drinking any milk after hearing this."

Ethan chose overlook her comments and continued. He took the rag and washed the animal's udder and teats. "After you've cleaned off the area, you wrap your thumb and first finger around her teat and gently pull and squeeze."

A stream of liquid hit the ground. "Always let the first few squirts go to waste. Check to make certain it's white and looks good. If she has a clogged teat or blood in the stream, we don't want to use that milk."

"You're making me gag."

"Pull up the stool and sit down."

"I don't want to do this."

"The stool is hanging on the wall behind you."

Finally, she reached over and pulled the wooden pedestal down. She placed the seat close to him. He turned to her. "You know, if you're not nervous, the cow enjoys being milked. It relieves the pressure from her udder. She'll thank you."

"She may be ecstatic, but I'm not."

Again, he didn't respond but rather waited patiently for her to accept she would soon be milking a cow. She sank down on the stool and tentatively reached out to touch the cow's teat. He saw her shudder and wondered at that moment if all city women were this squeamish. He'd been milking cows since he was seven. It was nothing, one of the easiest jobs on the ranch.

Placing her between his legs on the same stool, he wrapped his arms around her tiny body. With his hands over hers, he helped her squeeze.

Milk shot out of the teat, hitting the ground. She jumped. "Oh my. I did it."

"Now squeeze each teat just like that."

Her body fit his perfectly, as she rested against his chest Together, they clutched the animal's teats.

The cow turned and glanced at Beth, giving her a look that said, "You're new". Ethan patted the cow on the backside. "Good girl."

Once Beth had squeezed each of the four teats, he handed her a bucket. "Now, put the pail under the udder and clasp them two at a time."

"Oh, this is so icky. I'm touching an animal's breasts."

He laughed. "And she's enjoying it." And he was savoring Beth being in his arms, snug against him.

She looked up at him. "This isn't as bad as I'd feared."

"I told you," he said, breathing in deeply the scent of her hair. He wanted to place his mouth against her neck, but he was afraid she would jump and spook the animal. So instead, he barely moved, while he enjoyed the feel and the smell of her and marveled at this woman he'd married.

"When you made the decision to come to Colorado, what did you expect? Did you think it would be like living in Chicago?"

She inhaled deeply. "No. I just had to get out of Chicago."

Was that a slip or had she meant to admit her sudden need to leave? Suddenly, he understood why she had no bags, no clothes other than the ones on her back, and only a small valise that carried a few personal items. "So you ran?" he asked.

"Yes." Abruptly, she clammed up like she didn't want to talk about this anymore.

"Why?" he asked, curious as to what would make a strong woman like her leave an opulent lifestyle.

She sighed but continued milking the cow. "My wedding was in two days, and I knew I couldn't marry Henry."

Damn! She'd left another man to run straight into Ethan's arms, so he was competing with her ex-fiancé. Why couldn't his mother have minded her own business?

At that thought, the barn door opened and in walked the woman herself. "Ethan, I've been looking everywhere for you. A word, please."

~

Ethan finished showing Beth how to milk the cow then followed his mother out of the barn to the main house. He knew his mother meant business when she took him into her office and closed the door, which only made his hackles rise at the way she was treating him. He was not an errant schoolboy. He was a man who made decisions on his own, without her help.

She sank into the chair on the other side of the desk from him. Just when things were getting really interesting with his wife, his mother had interfered yet again.

Sitting across from her, he didn't say a word, only stared.

"Son, I know you're angry with me."

"Yes, I am, Mother," he replied.

"I know you haven't had as much time as your brothers to find a wife of your own, but I thought you were old enough to settle down."

After what his new wife had just told him, he was spitting mad all over again. "I'm a man, and I don't need you choosing for me. I almost walked away from this girl, and now, I'm beginning to wonder if that would have been the right move."

Hell, who was he kidding? Sure, she wasn't the woman he'd have picked to marry, but still, she was interesting, intriguing, and he was starting to understand more about her. And this stunning creature was his *wife*.

Nodding like she understood his anger, his mother folded her hands together on the top of the desk. "I wasn't going to make the same mistake with you I've made with your brothers. Caleb and Gideon should have been married a long time ago. You were starting to go down the same path as Caleb, and I wasn't going to stand by and watch you chase every skirt in town and not make a commitment to any of them."

The skin on the back of Ethan's neck tightened with alarm. Just because he was the youngest didn't mean he was walking the same path as his brothers. Didn't she hear what he'd said? "Again, I am my own man. I was not following in Caleb's footsteps."

"I was told when you go to town with your brother, you two spent time with loose women and drank."

"Did you ever consider we might be flirting with women? Sure, I went to Angel Springs on Saturday nights and enjoyed female company, but I was also courting a girl in town and had planned to ask her father if I could take her to dinner after the weather cleared. If you'd just waited, I would have found someone on my own. But instead, you jumped in and made the decision for me."

His mother frowned. "I didn't know."

"A man doesn't tell his mother everything. If he did, he's not much of a man. Why did you think it was such a good idea to order us brides? You do realize Beth has never taken care of herself. This woman doesn't even know how to make a bed." And she didn't want to learn from what he'd gathered so far. The woman had servants who took care of her every wish, and now she was here in the mountains with him—a man who could never give her that kind of life and didn't want to, even if he had more money than sense.

He wanted to throw this latest news in his mother's face but not until he had all the facts. Beth was running from a wedding, and that meant there was a fiancé somewhere who was wondering where his bride had gone.

Tears welled up in his mother's eyes, and Ethan groaned internally. Why did women think tears solved everything?

No, this time it wasn't going to work. He'd caved the first time she'd cried but not today. Today, he was taking a stand.

"Maybe, I was wrong, but I'm not always going to be here. I wanted to see all my sons married and maybe even more grandchildren. If I'd asked you boys in advance, you all would have told me no."

"And that's as it should be. We're men, Mama, not boys," Ethan answered, his anger fueling up again. "I've got to go. Are we done here?"

"Ethan," his mother said, wiping at her eyes.

"Stop trying to run my life, or I won't be in yours." He stood, needing to get away from her.

He wasn't ready to put this behind him. He had a wife who, though she was beautiful, wasn't exactly the type of woman he would have chosen to share his life with on the ranch.

His independence, his manhood, was on the line here, and until his mother conceded, he wasn't ready to forgive and forget.

~

The next morning, Beth stood outside the main house and watched her husband ride off with the other cowboys. The sun shone brightly, the temperature was above freezing, and the snow was beginning to turn to mush. There was talk of the road to town being passable again soon.

Any day now, Gideon and Ruby would be leaving to return to Angel Springs and his congregation.

Her fellow sisters-in-law were friendly to her, but she could see the condemnation in their eyes. They knew how to do the chores Mrs. Fraser had given them, but Beth, she knew nothing.

And their disapproval hurt.

In Chicago, she was known for holding fashionable teas with the debutantes and socialites, but here in Colorado, her self-worth was nothing. Zero. She was the object of ridicule, and Ethan was pitied by the cowpokes. Of all the brides who'd arrived, he'd been saddled with the worst, and that made her chest ache with sadness.

Even after she learned how to milk the cow, they gazed at her like "So what?" They'd been doing that simple chore all their life.

It wasn't her fault she'd been raised in the city, where women were catered to. Was it right to scorn her for being born into privilege and wealth, with servants who tended to her every need?

The other women made her feel like an outsider. That had never happened before in Beth's life, and she hated being the odd one.

The only good thing was Ethan. Still, he would look at her with that same reproach, but then he would try to show her what she needed to know. Just like the day he'd taught her how to milk the cow, he'd taken the time to teach her how to make the chickens give up their eggs and the proper way to feed the animals. Since they lived in the barn, it was her job to make certain the horses, the pigs, the chickens, and even those rascally goats had enough hay.

She sighed. Only a few more days, then she could buy her train ticket back to Chicago with the money from selling her brooch and leave all this behind. The plan had never been to stay, but rather to find a husband, obtain the marriage license, and hightail it back home, where she could gleefully show her father, *too late. I'm married and there is nothing you can do.*

"Beth, dear," Mrs. Fraser called from the front door. "Milly wants to know if you'd like to learn how to bake a cake today."

"Sure," she said, picking up her skirts and walking through the slush. The weather was bad enough, but the constant mixture of ice, snow, and mud was enough to send any woman running back to the city. The bottom of her skirt was ruined from being continuously wet; even her petticoat had a muddy stain.

Looking off in the distance, she saw the back of her husband, and her heart beat faster and her chest warmed. The man was decent, he was kind, and she liked the way he kissed. But that wasn't enough to make her stay at the Circle F. The mountains were beautiful, and even the snow was pretty, but she wanted to return home, back to where she belonged, where she was at the top of her social circle, not the one being ridiculed.

"Are you doing okay, dear?" Mrs. Fraser asked.

She sighed again. "I'm a little homesick today."

"Well, then, we just need to get you busy. When you're working, troubles seem to disappear."

Beth had to bite her lip to keep from snorting. Why did these people think work solved everything?

Walking into the kitchen, she found Milly waiting for her with the ingredients on the table. "Okay, Beth, the first thing I want you to do is combine the butter and sugar in this bowl here. Usually, I take my fork and whip it until the batter is nice and creamy."

For the next hour, Beth let Milly teach her how to bake. It wasn't that hard, and suddenly, she felt excited about showing Ethan what she'd done today, how she'd created the dessert for today's lunch.

As she slid the pans into the oven, she thought about the cows. "Did Clara milk the cows this morning?"

"I don't know," Milly said. "I never worry about it since my job is here in the kitchen."

"Oh dear, I'm supposed to be helping her. It's much quicker with two hands. I better go check."

Beth hurried out the door of the kitchen, crossing through the slushy snow to the barn. As she walked in, Clara had a cart and was pulling it to the house, filled with the pails of milk.

She frowned when she saw Beth striding toward her. "Where have you been, missy? It's taken me all morning to milk the cows. There's still the cream to separate and butter to make. If you're too good to help me, then I'll give the job to one of the other girls."

A feeling of shame came over Beth. She hadn't deliberately not helped Clara; it was just she'd become distracted at the idea of baking with Milly. "I'm sorry, Clara. Mrs. Fraser told me Milly would show me how to bake a cake. I just remembered the cows."

"You can't forget about the livestock. With their teats swollen with milk, we have to take care of them. Now help me get these pails to the house."

Taking a deep breath, Beth helped the older woman pull the cart, some of the milk sloshing over the side of the pails into the wagon. She tried to hold up her skirt as they trod through the slush. "What about the eggs?"

The older woman snorted. "I took care of them before the sun rose. Probably before you were out of bed."

Having risen before daylight, Beth let Clara's comments go. No matter how hard she tried, no one around here respected her. They all believed she was weak.

Glancing up, she watched as Ethan and the men returned. It was lunchtime, and they would eat then ride out again. He'd told her in the springtime they often left the ranch for days at a time, while they worked the cattle.

For some crazy odd reason, she wanted time alone with her husband, some time for the two of them to do something fun together. Maybe she could convince him they should go to town, maybe buy a new dress, and even check the train schedule. And just be the two of them together.

While she knew they wouldn't have forever, she was drawn to this man she'd married.

Spending time away in Angel Springs with her husband could do a lot to cheer her up and make her feel like a useful human being again.

"Ethan," she called as she and Clara reached the house. She waved to get his attention. "Clara, I'll be right in to help you. I just want to ask Ethan a question," she said.

"You make certain you come back," Clara called after her as Beth hurried across the yard to the barn, where the men were sliding off their horses.

The thought of spending time with her husband and riding into town had her eager to speak with him. She wanted them to make plans as to when they could get away. Maybe she could talk him into a couple of days in Angel Springs, with the two of them eating at restaurants, going to the theater, and doing some shopping. When she'd arrived, Pete had whisked them away from the train station so quickly she didn't remember much about Angel Springs, but hopefully even out west, there was entertainment.

Reaching Ethan, she noticed he was in a heated discussion with his brother.

"I've worked hard around this ranch, and this is the first time I've ever asked for anything. I think I'm owed."

"It's not a matter of you being owed. It's a matter of whether or not we have the funds and everyone agrees to spend the money on your project. You're going to have to wait and see."

Jamie and the other men walked away from Ethan, and she could tell her husband was angry. Maybe this wasn't the best time to ask him, but she couldn't help herself.

She rushed to him. "Hi," she said.

He glanced at her. "Hi." His tone was less than friendly, and she could tell he was tense. But that didn't slow her down.

"I heard the road is passable."

"No, the snow has stopped and is melting, but that doesn't mean we can get to town."

Disappointment filled her, causing her chest to ache as she realized she was stuck here. There was no escape from the people, the work, and most of all from her own lack of capabilities. "Oh," she said, trying to hide her despair, but she didn't let that slow her down, her need for something positive overwhelming her rationale. "I was thinking maybe in the next day or two, we could sneak off to town, just you and me. Spend a couple of days there. Do some shopping, see a play, eat at a couple of restaurants."

Shaking his head, he laughed. "Honey, the only entertainment in Angel Springs is the saloon, and I don't think you want to hang out there."

Stunned, she stared at him. "There's no theater? No plays?"

"The closest theater is in Denver."

Tears bubbled up inside her at how much she'd given up, the reality slamming into her, leaving her almost breathless. It had never occurred to her there wouldn't be any kind of opera house or any kind of social interaction, except with the people who despised her. "What do people do for entertainment?"

"Not much. Every so often, the Grange Hall holds a dance. I think there's one coming up in the next few weeks. We'll try to go."

This was not what she wanted to hear. She needed to get away from the ranch and feel like a normal human being again, like a refined woman, not some backwoods hillbilly stuck in the middle of nowhere.

She glanced down at her hands and saw how red and scaly they were. An urgent longing for her old way of life filled her body, rushing to her stomach like she'd eaten something bad. She wanted to go home. "But that's not for weeks."

He glanced at her, his eyes flashing with annoyance. "Just *why* did you come to Colorado?"

Now, even Ethan was beginning to have contempt for her. Soon he would hate her like the others.

"I told you I was running from a wedding."

"Did you ever consider what you were getting yourself into? Beth, this is our life. This is what you can expect every day. Nothing more. No fancy parties. No theaters or socials. Just hardworking folk taking care of the ranch, day in and day out."

Obviously, she hadn't contemplated what kind of life she was getting into when she'd run. All she could think about was leaving before her father forced her to marry a man who didn't want her, just her trust fund and a hostess for his parties. There would never have been love between the two of them.

"Thanks for telling me," she said, pain gathering like a storm in her chest as she turned and walked away to go to the bunkhouse to help Milly and Clara serve the noonday meal. Then she would help Clara skim the cream and churn the butter and slowly die inside.

Ethan probably regretted marrying her, and how could she blame him? She was not exactly the kind of woman a man like him needed. It would be better for him when she was gone. And at this moment, she was ready to go back where she belonged.

As she went into the bunkhouse the men were already at the table scarfing down the food put in front of them. She walked into the serving area. "Milly, where's the cake we made?"

Milly smiled sadly at her, and an uneasy feeling settled in the pit of Beth's stomach. "Beth, baking is an art, and for some people it takes several tries for them to feel comfortable in the kitchen. I firmly believe the ingredients know when a person is just starting or is nervous about the preparation."

A sense of foreboding overcame Beth. "Where's the cake?"

"I left it on top of the stove. It's not edible?."

She frowned. "Why not?"

"It fell, Beth."

"Fell?"

"Something went wrong. When I pulled it from the oven, there was no fluffy center, just mush."

Laughter roared through the dining room, and she heard someone say, "Beth's first cake."

Milly's eyes widened. "Oh no, did those men find that cake? I'm going to take a broom to their hide."

Together, she and Beth ran to the dining room door, where Spunky Barton, one of the hired hands, was holding the disastrous dessert up for everyone to see Beth's ill-fated creation. The men were laughing and slapping Ethan on the back.

"You're going to starve if that woman ever has to cook for you," Spunky declared.

She'd suffered enough at the hands of everyone on this ranch, and she refused to take it anymore. Enough already.

With her head held high, her heart crying inside, and her feet carrying her forward, Beth stoically walked over to the man, took the pan from him, and smashed the dessert in his face. "You try to make a cake and see if *you* can do any better."

She'd had enough of being the brunt of everyone's jokes. She was doing the best she could.

Stunned, Spunky stood there with yellow cake dripping off his face. "Gosh darn it, but that woman has some spunk."

Beth turned and walked out of the dining room, her head high, her back as rigid as the Rockies, with tears brimming on her lashes. They would not see her cry. Rapidly, she blinked them away.

Determined to reach the sanctity of the loft, she stepped out the door and took two steps. Her boot hit a patch of ice, sending her feet flying toward her head. With a splat, she went down. Ice-cold mud seeped through her dress into her pantaloons.

With an anguished cry, she looked out at the mountains and shook her fist. "I'm going home."

Picking herself up, she hurried toward the loft as fast as her feet would take her, knowing if the men came out and found her in the slush, they would get another laugh at her benefit.

To hell with all of them.

To hell with this drafty loft, the husband who was ashamed of her, and trying to change who she was.

She was Elizabeth Worthington, debutante, heir to one of the richest fortunes in Chicago, and she was returning to where she belonged. Today, right this minute, if possible. She was done.

Chapter Five

Beth went into the loft, gathered her few items, bundled up the best she could, and went down to where the men's horses were waiting while they ate their lunch. They stood munching some hay, saddled and ready to go. Quickly, she tied her items to the back of a docile looking mare and climbed up onto her back. Thank goodness her father had made certain she'd taken riding lessons when she was a child.

Kicking the mare, she rode out of the yard in the direction she remembered Angel Springs lay. Hurrying through the snow, she knew they were only about five miles from town. The snow was beginning to melt, the sun was shining, and the wind was blowing the drifts in different directions. How difficult could it be to ride a horse into the small village? If a man could do it, so could she.

Thirty minutes later, Beth regretted her hasty decision. The horse struggled to get through the drifts, some of them coming up to the animal's sternum. Snow swirled with the wind, making it difficult to see which direction she was headed. And on either side of her, the towering cliffs were bulging with the white powdery stuff.

Fear rushed at her like an avalanche.

And she had no idea if she was headed toward Angel Springs or wandering aimlessly in the high country.

Darkness had been falling when she rode to the ranch with the brides, and the snow had been blowing thick and heavy. The women had been talking excitedly about the men they were about to meet. Beth hadn't paid attention to the direction of the road. Right now, she could be lost and wouldn't even realize how dire her situation was until it was too late.

Her mare snorted and halted, the animal refusing to move when Beth kicked her sides. She didn't understand what was spooking the animal. And that frightened her even more. What if it was a mountain lion or a wolf or an outlaw? What had she been thinking to ride out of the safety of the ranch into a white wilderness she knew nothing about?

She couldn't go back and face all of them in humiliation. She urged the horse forward. She whined, but began to move. "Come on, girl. Just get me to town, and I'll make sure there are some nice oats waiting for you."

"Beth!" A man's voice called her name.

She refused to look back. She was not returning no matter how frozen her feet were or that her pantaloons had frozen to the saddle.

"Stop, Beth!" Ethan called. "You're in danger. You could trigger an avalanche any second with the way the snow is piled up on those cliffs. Slowly back your horse out of that canyon."

What was he talking about? It was only snow.

The horse's foot slipped on something and made a clunking noise that echoed through the canyon. A cracking noise like ice splintering resounded around her.

"Beth, stop the horse! Now! The snow on the side of those cliffs is about to fall."

His voice was commanding. Her teeth were chattering, her feet were numb with the cold, yet she wanted to continue. She wanted to reach town and get away, but fear had her pulling up on the reins. She brought the horse to a halt, disappointment crushing her chest, rushing through her, making her even colder. She wasn't going home today.

Turning around, she glanced behind her at Ethan. He'd come after her.

"Back your horse up real slow and easy."

Why wasn't he entering the canyon and coming after her?

Tugging on the reins, she squeezed softly with her legs, and the horse began walk backward. She continued for about six feet. Then suddenly Ethan grabbed her reins. He pulled her the rest of the way out of the canyon, until they were in an open area away from the danger.

"What the hell do you think you're doing?"

"I was going home. Back to where I'm not the object of everyone's jokes. That way you won't be ashamed of your wife."

Ethan cursed as he stared at her. It was the first time she'd ever heard him use swear words. "If you hadn't rushed out of there with your tail on fire, you would have heard me defending you. You would have seen me pick up a piece of that cake from the floor, eat it, and tell Spunky he was missing out on the mighty fine dessert my wife made."

Leaping from his saddle, he held onto the reins of her horse as he dragged her from her horse. She slid off, her legs sinking almost thigh deep into the snow. "Don't you ever try to go to town after a snowstorm again. This canyon is a huge avalanche danger that could swallow you up, and we wouldn't find your body until spring."

The cracking noise echoed through the canyon, and they watched in horror as snow rushed from the cliffs down to the floor of the gorge where Beth's horse had halted.

Ethan cursed and wrapped his arms around her. "I almost lost you."

He'd saved her life.

She began to shake. The cold seeped through her skirt, leaving her wet. "I'm…sorry," she said. "I didn't know about the danger. This is so different from my life in Chicago. I'm trying, Ethan. I'm really trying, but I've gone from being a popular debutante to someone everyone ridicules."

"I know you are, Beth. I can see that. One of these days we'll look back and laugh at this, but don't ever think I'm ashamed of you. I'm very proud of the fact you're my wife."

She was trembling so hard with the cold that even his body heat wasn't enough to warm her.

"Let's get you home. You're almost frozen."

Instead of putting her back on her horse, he helped her onto his. Tying her reins to his saddle, he climbed up behind her. "I thought this would be warmer. Your lips are blue."

"Thanks," she managed to mumble. Her brain felt like it was moving in slow motion. Everything seemed to be a blur, and she leaned back against Ethan, fighting drowsiness.

Kicking his horse, he got them moving into a steady trot that rocked her gently in his arms.

Suddenly, he was shaking her. "Don't you go to sleep. You're too cold."

She tried to speak, but her lips felt frozen, her toes and fingers no longer had any feeling in them, and sleep seemed peaceful.

"You know I wasn't lying when I said the cake was delicious. Sure, it had fallen, but the flavor was good and sweet. What are you going to make for me next?"

Licking her lips, she tried to talk. "Mud pie."

His laughter rumbled in his chest against her back. "Now, there's a pie you could have thrown in Spunky's face."

A snort came from her, and she shook her head, trying to clear the fog from her brain. "He deserved that dessert in his face."

"Oh honey, if you could have seen his expression, it would warm you all the way to your toes. I doubt he makes fun of your cooking again."

What did it matter? She could have baked the best cake in the world, and they would have found another reason to taunt her. She was different than the rest of the women, yet all she wanted was to belong.

Finally, after what felt like forever, they reached the barn.

Mrs. Fraser came running from the house. "You found her."

"Yes, she was just about to go through Miller's Canyon."

"Oh no," the woman said. "That's where Jamie's first wife, Lucy, died."

"Yes, I know," Ethan said, swinging his leg over the side of his horse and sliding to the ground. He reached up and lifted Beth from the saddle.

Beth didn't say anything to Mrs. Fraser. Whatever strength she'd had was gone. She felt limp, almost lifeless, and as cold as a fisherman on the Great Lakes in winter.

"Please take care of the horse," Ethan said to his mother as he carried Beth into the barn.

"Put me down," she said weakly. "I can walk."

"No."

Dang, her husband could be demanding when he got angry. Leaning her head against his shoulder, she relaxed and let him carry her up the stairs and into their cozy loft—the place she'd hoped never to return to, yet she felt safe within this small confined area. The smells could be a little outrageous at times, but it was comfy.

Inside, he let her feet fall to the floor but held on to her. "Let's get you out of these wet clothes." He started unbuttoning her dress.

She pushed his hands aside. "I can do it." But her fingers were numb, and after several attempts, he took over.

"Has anyone ever told you how stubborn you are?"

She shook her head. "They wouldn't dare."

"Well, let me be the first."

A giggle escaped. Her dress fell to the floor, and she stood before him in her petticoats and chemise, which were soaking wet.

"Sorry, honey, but these have got to go."

"I'll take them off," she said, and before he could object, she quickly removed her petticoat, leaving just her pantaloons and chemise. She was shaking so hard she could barely talk. All she wanted was a warm bed.

"No, everything."

"I'm not getting naked," she said.

"Yes, you are."

"No, I'm not."

"Either you remove your clothes or I will," he said. "They're wet and you're freezing."

At this moment, she no longer had the strength to fight him, and frankly, she didn't care any longer. She was past the point of worrying about her dignity, her modesty, and even her reputation. She was married. And here in Colorado, she had no respectability.

"Oh, all right." She whirled her back to him and stripped completely naked. With two steps, she dove into the bed beneath the covers. "I'm claiming the bed."

His laughter filled the room, making it feel cozy, sending heat pulsing into her cold limbs. "It doesn't matter because I'm joining you."

"Oh no," she said, her teeth chattering.

From beneath the covers, she watched him throw a few more logs into the potbelly stove. Along the wall, he pulled out a narrow rope and strung it close to the fire where he hung her clothes to dry. When he finished, he stripped down to his long johns and crawled in bed with her.

"What are you doing? It's not night."

"No, but it's evening, and you're freezing. Until you stop shivering, this is where I'll be." He wrapped his arms around her, pulling her naked body in close.

The day's events suddenly overwhelmed her, and she realized how close she'd come to dying, trying to get back to the life she'd left. A life that was more show than reality.

Now that she realized the danger, she started to shake. She'd risked everything to get back to Chicago. She was stuck until a horse could pass through the canyon safely, and she had no idea when that would happen. Tears welled up in her eyes and slipped down her cheeks. She tried to hide them from Ethan, but he pulled her tighter and kissed her naked shoulder.

"You're safe and soon you'll be warm," he said gently.

But was she really safe? She was lying naked in her husband's arms, vulnerable. She expected he would soon take advantage of her weakened state and want sex. How could she deny him? They were married, and he'd just saved her life. With a sigh, she realized she'd probably give in to Ethan.

His hand was just below her breasts, and she could feel the heat from his body rapidly warming her. How could she have imagined that night she'd found her fiancé doing something so unthinkable that running from a wedding would send her straight into the arms of another man? And why did Ethan's arms feel so right?

~

For the first time in their married life, Ethan was sharing the bed with his wife. No, it wasn't the ideal situation, but seeing her today in the middle of that canyon that was known for avalanches had scared him enough, he wondered at the emotions that were churning through him. And seeing Spunky make fun of Beth had sent anger rushing through his blood like the raging rivers during spring snow melt. What was happening for him to experience so many emotions when his wife was around?

Was this how his father had felt with regard to his mother? Were his brothers just as confused about their wives? It wasn't love, but he wanted to protect her, keep her safe, and make her happy. And he was doing a lousy job.

Since they'd married, Beth had been having a hard time. He knew she wasn't a girl who was used to living on a ranch, and she was quickly learning not everyone had servants and a big house, the way she had back in Chicago. If she'd made it to town today, he knew she would have caught the next train home and left him behind.

And no matter what happened, Ethan was determined to make this marriage work. He didn't want to lose Beth. They'd been married less than a week, that was hardly enough time to get to know his bride.

The loft had darkened, and he hadn't bothered to light any lamps. For once, he decided his brothers could take care of the ranch without him. What he needed to concentrate on was making certain Beth was cocooned in the safety of his arms and remained warm.

"You're no longer trembling," he whispered in her ear.

"No, thank you," she said drowsily.

"Tell me about the life back in Chicago you miss so much."

She sighed but didn't move from his arms and he was glad. Nothing in this world could feel better than her naked body against his. And though he would like nothing more than to caress every inch of her smooth, silky skin, he knew now was not the right time. She needed whatever strength she had left to fight off the cold.

"My father is George Theodore Worthington, and he owns one of the largest banks in town—the Worthington Bank and Loan Company"

Shock gripped his innards, twisting them into a knot. He knew she was wealthy, but he had no idea just how much. Good grief, even the name sounded like old family money. No wonder she was used to servants and a finer way of life.

"So, why would a rich, society girl like you decide to come out West?"

"Because I didn't want to marry the man my father had chosen for me."

Ethan's chest tightened. Maybe now she'd tell him about the fiancé. About what had sent her running from her wedding. Did she still love this man?

"Why not?"

It was torture laying here, holding her in his arms, unable to touch her, but he wanted to spend this time with the two of them talking, getting to know each other. They really hadn't had the opportunity to learn about one another, and maybe it was time he started giving more to this marriage. It was forever.

"I wish I could say he was a big fat old bore, but he wasn't. He was a nice man, a little older than I would have preferred, but all right. He was my father's friend."

You would think Ethan would feel jealous at the mention of her fiancé, but there was something about the way she described him that let Ethan know right away she held no romantic feelings for the older gentleman. And in some ways, he felt the need to pity the poor man for losing what Ethan had gained.

"You say he was all right like you're talking about the weather being fine. Didn't you love him?"

She laughed softly in the darkness. "In a marriage where the merging of funds is the important factor, love is not part of the equation, only how much this union will increase your wealth. And if we'd married and had children, they would have been equal to if not richer than the Vanderbilts."

Stunned, he lay beside her, trying to calculate how much wealth she'd walked away from. But there was a bigger question. "And you walked away from it all. Why?"

With a shrug, she said, "I didn't love him."

But she hadn't loved Ethan when she arrived, and he even doubted she loved him at this moment. There was something she was hiding. Today, he'd let it go, but eventually he wanted to know the real reason she'd run from her fiancé.

She paused for a moment. "What about you? Wasn't there a girl in town you were sweet on? Someone you were planning to marry?"

"There was," he said. "But my mother took care of that for me."

Beth rolled in his arms and gazed up at him in the darkness. "I'm sorry. Our marriage ended that for you."

He kept his arm around her and pulled her up next to him. She laid her head on his shoulder, and he couldn't help but think she was killing him. His johnson was hard and begging for release, but he ignored the craving of his body, hoping to at last form a union with his wife.

"It wasn't that serious. We'd been talking. That's all." The image of Alyssa came to mind, and he felt bad. He'd not returned to town to let her know he'd gotten married. Somehow he felt like he at least owed her an explanation. She'd been a pretty girl, but it hadn't been meant to be.

"What were you and your brother arguing about today?"

He sighed. "I told him that since we're married, we deserved a house, the same as the rest of them. He told me the family has to vote on the decision, and it would be decided by whether or not we had a good season."

"You were trying to get us a house?"

"Yes, I told you when we married living in the barn wouldn't last forever."

She wrapped her arms around him. "Thank you."

She didn't seem as excited as he'd expected her to react, but then maybe she was exhausted from her ordeal. Or could it be she was hiding something?

Quickly, he pushed the thought away, not wanting to believe she would be dishonest with him. Trust was such a fragile thing between two people, and she was the person he wanted to believe in.

Ethan reached over and ran his hand down her cheek. "You deserve better than living in a loft. I'll do my best to convince my brother we need that house."

Reaching out, she tentatively placed her lips on his. His groin tightened as his mouth needed no further invitation, and he covered her lips, his tongue stroking the inside of her mouth. She was so sweet and innocent one moment, and the next she could be a firebrand, sizzling with impertinence.

No, tonight was not the night to make her his, but he was going to do everything he could to make her feel accepted, to court her in his own way. Pay attention to her, do something special for her. He was going to do everything he could to make her want him.

Breaking off the kiss, he asked, "Are you getting warmer?"

"Yes," she said breathlessly. "You know, this is very cozy."

Not exactly the word he was looking for, but at least he'd been given a second chance to make this marriage work. And he would do everything he could to ensure Beth was his wife in every sense of the word. Soon…very soon.

"Sleep," he said. "You need the rest. I'll hold you and keep you warm all night long."

~

Shadows filled the loft when Beth awoke the next morning with Ethan's arms around her. She'd slept naked next to him all night long. His body heat had warmed her through the long hours until dawn.

She sighed and didn't move, not wanting to wake him. She'd expected he would try to make love to her, but instead, he'd simply held her, making certain she stayed snug and cozy. And now she was more confused than ever.

They were married, and his reaction to her nakedness had been long and hard against her backside, yet he'd waited. Ethan Fraser was turning out to be quite an enigma. He was different from any man she'd ever met, and she found herself really liking the cowboy. But her plans hadn't changed. They were still to get to town and return to Chicago as a married woman.

"You awake?" he asked softly, kissing her bare shoulder.

"Yes," she whispered in the darkness.

"Good. How do bacon and eggs sound this morning?" he asked.

Her stomach growled at the mention of food. They'd missed dinner last night and were probably too late for the bunkhouse meal. In fact, she was late getting to the animals.

She sighed. Back to work today.

"I need to tend to the animals. Clara will be upset with me if I don't get down there." She started to rise out of bed, but his hand halted her.

"No, this morning we're taking time for us. I'll help you with the animals and join the men later."

She rolled over and smiled at him. "Thanks, Ethan. And thanks for coming to my rescue yesterday."

The cold had sapped her, frozen her, before she'd realized what had happened, but the scariest thing had been the avalanche. A moment longer and that mountain of snow would have rumbled down on top of her. She shivered at the memory.

He pulled her into his arms. "Just don't do that kind of thing again. You scared me."

His lips found hers, and he kissed her, his mouth moving over hers with a tenderness that had her pressing against him, wanting, needing more.

Abruptly, he broke off the kiss. In the darkness, his brown eyes were dilated as he stared at her. "We better get up, or we're going to spend all day right here in this bed, doing what married folks enjoy."

Her cheeks flamed, and she smiled as warmth traveled through her nether regions. The thought wasn't a bad one and that surprised her. She was trying to get back to Chicago, not become further entangled with her husband. "Your mother would come check on us."

"My mother knows better than to come to the loft."

As she rolled over to get out of bed, he swatted her playfully on the behind, and she giggled. The man was touching her naked butt, and it didn't seem awkward. It felt right, even though he'd never seen her body in the light before. There was a relaxed ease between them this morning that yesterday had not existed, and she felt comfortable with him.

"Uh, if you want to go behind the screen, I'll hand you your clothes," he said. "And I'll even turn my back for about ten seconds."

"That's not long enough," she said, lying on her side with the covers clutched to her chest.

"Yeah, I know," he replied with a smile.

She laughed at the outrageousness of Ethan and couldn't believe she was happy, even playful with her husband. "Turn your back."

"I'm ready for us to get past this part of being newlyweds."

But that was the problem. They would never get past this part of being newlyweds because soon she would be on a train headed back to Chicago with proof she could no longer be forced to marry anyone she didn't want to because she was already a married woman.

"Not yet," she said and scurried out of the bed, running across the cold wooden floor to the screen.

Even before she reached the partition, she heard him rustling about in the bed. "You better not be peeking," she called out.

They were playing with fire, and she feared if they continued this flirting, someone was going to get burned. And she didn't want to hurt Ethan; he'd been kind to her. He'd rescued her, and someday she owed him an explanation as to why their marriage would never work.

"I promise you I am. That's a mighty fine backside you have, Mrs. Fraser."

"Ethan, you cheated."

"Of course I did. I'm a man. You're my wife. I want to see what I married."

She smiled from behind the partition. His words created heat that seared her all the way to her toes, yet he made her feel special, and that could be a problem. While Ethan was a wonderful man, she could not let her emotions become involved with her husband. It just wasn't possible.

"You know I may just keep your clothes. You'd have to come out and get them off the line."

"You wouldn't. You promised you'd bring them to me."

Yet here they were bantering like two people courting, and it felt right. Ethan felt right, and that disturbed her because she couldn't stay, and she was certain he wouldn't belong in Chicago any more than she belonged here.

Just then, he laid her clothes over the top of the partition. "Next time, you're going to have to come get them."

"Ha. We'll just see about that."

Living with Ethan she was learning could be fun. He liked to tease her and she tried to give back as much as he dished out, but taunting her about her clothes was dangerous. If she wanted to walk out of here a virgin, he didn't need to see her naked.

Donning the hated dress she'd worn for days, she realized she'd. soon, be running around in threads. The old dress was already showing signs of wear and tear. Even her servants at home dressed better than this rag. But she didn't want to ask for one of Mrs. Fraser's gowns. They just weren't up to her standards.

She could hear and smell frying bacon and when she came out from behind the screen, Ethan was cooking eggs.

"Isn't it dangerous to have a potbelly stove in a barn?"

The heat was lovely, but she couldn't help but feel concerned for the animals down below, especially her cows. They weren't her cows, but she worried about them just the same.

Startled, she realized she was concerned about the animals. Her ladies needed her. What a change from a few days ago.

"Yes, but if you notice, it's on the wall away from where the animals are kept. The tack room and my woodworking shop are directly beneath us. The hay is stored in a separate lean-to attached to the barn, to try to minimize fire danger. But once we get our own home, we'll probably remove the stove."

She wanted to help him, but she didn't really know what to do.

As if he sensed her dilemma, he said, "Why don't you get us a couple of plates and forks out of that cabinet hanging on the wall. The coffee cups are there as well."

Ethan kept a tidy living space, and she'd been shocked to see how clean the kitchen area was and how neatly everything was arranged. But then again, he liked things orderly. And even had on occasion fussed at her to pick up her clothing. Not that she had that many. At home, Maria took care of all that. Beth had never had to tidy up.

"Is there any tea?" she asked.

He smiled and his face lit up sending warmth through her. "No, we'll have to get some the next time we're in town."

Opening the cabinet, she found the plates and handed them to him. "How come you know how to cook?" She wanted to know how he'd learned. Most men didn't know a thing about what went on in the kitchen, yet there were a few who functioned quite well. Ethan seemed at ease.

"Whenever we go on trail rides and at branding time, we stay out in the field. Someone has to cook, and usually the oldest and the youngest are in charge of the meals. By the time I was ten, I knew how to cook eggs, beans, and a rack of beef over a campfire. But don't ask me how to bake a cake."

The memory of her disastrous dessert from yesterday came rushing back. How could she ever look at Spunky again? She'd humiliated the man in front of his coworkers and friends. He must hate her for what she'd done. But she also wondered if Ethan had told her the truth or had he just wanted to make her feel better? "Did you really eat a piece of that cake off the floor or were you just being nice?"

He set a plate of eggs and bacon in front of her. "Yes, I ate a piece of your cake, not because I was being nice, but because you're my wife and it's my job to defend you. That cake tasted damn good."

Pride filled her. Maybe yesterday's cooking hadn't been a complete fiasco. Maybe she should try again. But just not with a cake. She wasn't ready to take on that challenge again so soon.

Taking a bite of egg, she smiled at him realizing even though the cake had not risen, it had tasted good. Even though they'd made fun of her, it wasn't as bad as she'd been led to believe. Ethan had defended her and that brought joy to her heart. "Thank you."

"Today, after you finish with the animals, I think you should get back in that kitchen and bake again."

She shook her head, the memory still too fresh in her head of how they'd laughed at her attempt. "No, I think maybe I'll start with something smaller. How about some cookies? Do you have a favorite kind?"

"Oatmeal or sugar cookies or anything you decide to fix."

How in the world could she hurt him so badly when he was doing so much to make her fit into his world and to help her feel wanted? And she planned to repay him by running away, leaving him alone, without a wife.

Guilt ate at her insides like the hunger she'd felt earlier, but she couldn't stay and live this kind of life. This was not what she wanted. She couldn't stay and be a rancher's wife, Ethan's wife.

Chapter Six

After breakfast, Beth and Ethan walked down the stairs into the barn, where he helped her catch up on her chores. "Does everyone know I left yesterday?"

"Only my mother, Caleb, and me." Ethan brushed his roughened hand against hers as they milked the cow together. "Our business is our business and not open for discussion with the family. I asked them not to say anything."

"I'm surprised you didn't say something to the hands," she said, pushing the cow's back leg away from her.

"It was none of their business," he said in a rough voice. "Telling mother was hard enough."

"You're still angry with her, aren't you?" Beth said, squeezing the animal's teats. Though it was work, she enjoyed his company. She liked being around Ethan, but her life was back in Chicago.

"There comes a time in a person's life when they become a man or a woman, and their parents cease to make decisions for them. That time has long since come for me, and my mother is still making decisions for me and interfering. I'm putting a halt to it now."

Beth thought about his comment and wondered how she could heal this rift between Ethan and his mother. Then she thought about her own parent and how he'd made the wrong decisions for her. She'd blindly gone along with him until that fateful night right before the wedding.

"I'm glad you're standing up to your mother. I didn't stand up for myself," she said quietly, her chest aching at the realization she'd been just as much to blame. "I didn't love Henry. Deep inside I knew he wouldn't be a good groom for me, but I agreed to the plans for the biggest society wedding of the year. I was so caught up with the idea of a fancy wedding I forgot about what really mattered in a marriage."

Ethan stopped milking, stood, and walked around to her. She put lubricant on each one of the cow's teats and stood. He waited for her. "So tell me what you think is important in a marriage."

She hung up the milking stool, while Ethan picked up the milk pails and put them in the cart. Wiping her hands on a rag, she glanced at him. "I think love is the most important element in a good marriage, but along with that, you need trust, friendship, and a partnership to work together."

"I'm glad you didn't love Henry," Ethan said.

The idea of love had never entered into her relationship with her father's friend. They were business acquaintances. She was an acquisition for a rich older man. Only, she'd seen things she should never have witnessed and gotten spooked and ran.

"Oh no," she said, shaking her head. "He didn't love me either. Oh, he went through all the right motions—flowers, jewelry, presents—but that's not real love. He was trying to buy my affections, and for a while, it worked."

Just then, the barn door opened and in strolled Clara. "There you are. I was beginning to think you'd forgotten to milk the cows again."

Ethan frowned at her. "Beth had a rough night. I helped her get the milking done, so it wouldn't be late." The older woman gazed at Beth, her head tilted sideways as she stared at her eyes making certain she wasn't ill. "You feeling okay?"

Beth was perfectly fine this morning. Embarrassed and even a little ashamed of how she'd treated Spunky, plus disappointed she hadn't reached town, but today was a new day. There would come a time when she tried to leave again. "I'm all right. After I finish up in here, I'm going to see Milly. I'd like to spend some time baking again."

"Allrighty, I'll just get these to the kitchen and get started." The older woman pulled the cart out of the barn, leaving Beth and Ethan alone again.

"I better go find the men and get started."

"Yeah," she said. "Thanks for helping me."

"You're welcome." He stood there, staring at her, not moving, and she knew he had something to say that was important.

Already she knew Ethan Fraser was not a man who gushed on about his emotions, but when he had something to say, it was wise to listen.

Clearing his throat nervously, he said, "Beth, I know we married before we knew each other, but I want to promise you I'll try my best to be a good husband to you. To make you happy."

Her husband was a good man. She smiled, believing in him, but unable to return his declaration. Part of her wanted to make a promise to him, but she knew she couldn't without lying. She wouldn't be here to be a good wife to him. "Thank you, Ethan."

He leaned in and gave her a quick kiss on the lips. Then he walked to the door of the barn. "But I'm not promising I'll give you your clothes again. I kind of liked seeing your naked butt sprinting across the room."

"Ethan Fraser," she called, unable to keep the smile off her face.

"See you tonight," he said, grinning as he disappeared out the door.

Warmth like the hottest rays of the sun flooded her body, and she raised her hands to her lips. She'd been kissed before, but no man had ever made her lips tingle and her female parts tremble. Whatever was in Ethan's caress was more potent than the finest wine, and she liked him kissing her.

~

Beth walked outside the barn and watched her husband riding off to find the men. The sun was shining brightly, but she knew how that cold wind could chill your innards before you realized you were nearly frozen. For the first time she understood how dangerous it was for the men to be out riding, taking care of the cattle. If they were caught in a snowstorm, their lives were in danger.

At the thought of Ethan in danger, her lungs froze, and she struggled to take a deep breath. He'd been doing this for a long time, and he'd return to her tonight, she reassured herself.

Hurrying through the slush, she glanced past the barn to the pigpens and saw Cat, Jamie's young daughter, climbing up on the fence, watching the pigs. "Cat, come away from there, honey."

At four years of age, Jamie's little girl was precocious and into all kinds of trouble. She hated wearing a dress, and Olivia was trying to convince her she'd look pretty in one, but so far, no interest.

"Why?" the young girl asked, climbing down and coming to Beth's side.

"They're big animals and can be dangerous."

"Oh," she said. "But I like to watch them feed their babies. That one mother pig, her teats are dragging on the ground."

Beth shook her head. At that age, she probably hadn't even known what a pig was, let alone that the animal had teats that could feed her piglets. At that age, she could only remember playing with her dolls.

"The sac is full of milk," she explained to the child. Cat probably already knew that, but Beth knew at least that much to tell the little girl.

"Oh," she said, walking alongside Beth. "What are you doing?"

"I'm going to help Clara make butter and strain the cream," Beth said. She didn't want to mention the word cookies because she didn't want the young girl to see how inadequate Beth was as a cook. And she didn't want to promise Cat sweets then come up with nothing.

"That's not fun," the little girl said.

Beth laughed. "I don't disagree with you, but I do like the taste of butter on my biscuits and in my cooking."

"Hmmm, hot buttered biscuits. Olivia makes us biscuits for breakfast," the child said then sighed and rolled her eyes. "She doesn't want me to wear boys' clothing. Said I should dress like a girl. Well, look at your skirts. They're muddy and my pants are tucked into my boots. They're not wet."

The statement was almost enough to make Beth go back into the barn and find an old pair of Ethan's pants and a shirt and put on. The child was right about dragging skirts in the mud. It got old quickly.

"Maybe you should ask her if you can wear boys' clothing around the ranch, but when you go into town, then you could wear dresses. You know, soon you're going to grow up, and boys will stare at you. You'll want to look pretty."

The child screwed up her face and said adamantly, "No boys."

Smiling, Beth hoped Cat kept that sentiment for as long as possible. Boys of any age only seemed to complicate your life.

They walked in silence for a few moments until they reached the kitchen.

"Can I help you with the butter?" the little girl asked.

"Cat Fraser," Olivia yelled from their home over the rise.

The little girl's eyes widened. "Oh no, I'm in trouble."

"For what?"

"I didn't put the dishes away," she said. "That's one of my chores. She makes me work."

"It's hard doing everything people tell you to do," Beth agreed.

"Yes." The child looked at Beth like she'd found someone who understood her. "I wanted to go outside, so I did when she wasn't looking."

"You know, there are other things I'd rather be doing, but I have to help out around the ranch. It takes all of us to keep it running," Beth responded to the child, hoping she was helping Olivia out, so the child would understand.

The little girl frowned at Beth then glanced back toward her home. "I better go. She's calling me."

"It was nice chatting with you, Cat," Beth said, and watched as the child splashed through the snow and mud, running as fast as her short little legs would carry her back to her home.

Beth opened the door to the bunkhouse and walked into the kitchen, where Milly greeted her. "Back to try again?"

"I'm not giving up on learning how to cook. I can do this," Beth said with confidence.

The older woman smiled at her. "Let's try something a little easier. I've been hankering for some sugar cookies. Do you want to give it a try?"

"Yes," Beth said, dragging down the same bowls she'd used yesterday to bake the cake.

"I'm really sorry Spunky found your cake. That man is always sneaking into the kitchen looking for sweets."

"It's okay," Beth replied, mixing the butter and eggs. She'd wondered if Milly was in on humiliating her, but now she knew the woman had been just as surprised. "I don't think he'll make fun of my cooking again."

Milly laughed. "Honey, I don't think any of them will make fun of your cooking."

Beth didn't feel proud of how she'd acted yesterday with Spunky, but enough was enough. It was hard learning to fit into this environment without being made the object of ridicule. And she'd reached her breaking point.

An hour later, she slid the final pan of cookies into the oven. She'd tasted the first batch, and even Milly had complimented her and told her they were delicious. Thrilled she'd finally had a success at cooking, she wanted to try more.

"Milly, what are you fixing for supper tonight?"

"Pork chops, mashed potatoes, and canned green beans from the garden," she said. "Why?"

"Would you let me fix Ethan's and mine?" Beth asked. "I want to surprise him."

The woman raised her brows. "Okay."

"Can I take the pork chops and fix them at our place? I mean, I'll watch you here then go over to the loft and fix it on the potbelly stove."

After Ethan had rescued her yesterday, she wanted to do something special for him. It would be great if he came home to his dinner ready and waiting for him. If she watched Milly, how hard could it be to copy her over at the loft?

"I don't know if that stove is going to be a great place to cook. I mean you can't really regulate the heat like I can here."

"I want to try. Ethan fixed me bacon and eggs this morning, and I want to do the same for him."

So far, Ethan had been the one to take care of her in their marriage. She wanted to do something for him. She wanted to be the one who he appreciated, not the other way around for a change.

Milly shook her head. "Okay, just don't burn down the loft, or you'll be sleeping over in the main house with Mrs. Fraser. And we all know how she and Ethan are not exactly getting along."

"I know. I feel bad about it, but Ethan has to be his own man," Beth said.

"And Mrs. Fraser is a mother who wants to make certain all of her children are taken care of. You'll understand someday very soon."

"Oh no," Beth said urgently at the realization they expected her to soon be pregnant.

"Happens to the best of us," Milly said, walking away.

There was no way she would bring a baby into this world to live up in a loft, although it wasn't a bad place. The smells were only occasionally noticeable, and the animals were mostly quiet. But her place was back in Chicago, amongst the upper echelon of society, not on a ranch in Colorado.

Chapter Seven

Ethan opened the door of the loft, and his eyes widened at the sight of flames shooting up from the top of the potbelly stove. Quickly, he ran over and placed the metal cover over the top, smothering the out of control fire.

Beth sank to the floor and looked at her pork chops now scattered across the rug, frustration filling her eyes.

"What happened?" he asked, getting a really bad feeling about his wife cooking alone in the loft. She wasn't ready to be turned loose with a skillet just yet.

She looked up at him, her large hazel eyes brimming with tears. "I was fixing us pork chops for dinner as a surprise. I was having trouble getting them to cook evenly. I turned my head for one second to set the table, and when I turned around, there was fire shooting to the ceiling." She sighed. "I grabbed the hot pan from the fire without using a pad. When I touched the hot handle, I dropped the pan."

Kneeling down, he reached for her hand. "Did you burn yourself?"

She gave him her hand, and already he could see the blisters forming. It could have been so much worse, but still, burning her hand had to hurt.

"Ouch. Let's put some salve on those blisters," he said, leading her out the door and down the stairs to the barn area.

Tears rolled down her cheeks and he sighed. If only women would save the weeping for things that really mattered.

"Quit crying. It's only food," he said. "It's not important."

"Yes, but I wanted to make you a nice dinner."

"And I appreciate that, but things sometimes happen. It's all right. I'm just thankful you weren't hurt any worse, and we still have a place to live."

The sight of flames reaching the ceiling had given his heart a jolt. "That stove is not easy for even the most seasoned cooks, so I'm surprised Milly let you try to cook on it."

"She warned me, but I wanted to try anyway."

The woman could be stubborn. He was seeing this more and more, and she would do just about anything to get her way, yet he liked her *I'm not going to give up* spirit. It probably was what had kept her alive the other day. It was dangerous and reckless and independent and wild. She was like a young mustang that needed to be tamed.

"I baked cookies today. They turned out real good," she whispered, as he lathered her hand in salve.

He smiled at her, trying to cheer her up. "We'll have cookies for dinner."

She giggled. "We have mashed potatoes if they didn't burn."

"Uh, I wouldn't count on them being edible. They were brown and stuck to the bottom of the pan."

"Oh," she said. "What about the green beans?"

He shook his head. "I'm sure the pigs will enjoy them."

She sighed, her head dropping to her chest.

He lifted her chin with his fingers. "How about I take you out for a steak?"

Her brows drew together. "What?"

"We'll eat at this fancy place I know, and they have really good steaks." He'd wanted to court his wife and spend some alone time with her, and now he knew how. He knew just the place where they could spend time gazing at the stars and cuddling together. Maybe if he were lucky, tonight would be the night she would give in and let them become man and wife in every sense of the word.

"Where?"

"I'll take you there," he said, lifting her by her good hand. They walked up the stairs together. When they reached the loft, he picked the pork chops off the floor, grabbed a blanket out of a cedar chest, and handed it to Beth. Then he took the burned food and put it all in a pan along with the pork chops.

"Get the cookies and your jacket," he called to her. If only he had a bottle of wine, but the only liquor they had was the hard stuff, and he wasn't going to give that to his wife.

Her gaze was filled with confusion as she followed him back down the stairs, pulling on her coat. "Where are we going?"

"To a fancy steak house."

Walking outside, they traipsed through the slush, which was starting to freeze once again, to the pigpen. Climbing up on the fence, he tossed the ruined supper out to the animals who squealed with delight and started snorting and grunting over the leftovers.

"See, they like it," he said.

"That's because they'd eat anything."

"Maybe, but they enjoyed that meal," he teased her as he grabbed her by the hand, and they started to walk to his favorite place on the ranch. This is where he went to get away from everything, and now he would share it with Beth.

"Where is this fancy steak house?"

Smiling at the confusion on her face, he said, "Come on. I'll show you."

They walked through the snow to a three-sided lean-to that held hay. There was a ladder leading to the top that was only about six feet off the ground. Ethan threw the blanket up then helped Beth climb the ladder, following closely behind her.

When they reached the top, she glanced out at the pasture. "Why are we here?"

No, it wasn't the best place to eat in Angel Springs, but the view would be beautiful, secluded, and unique. He hoped Beth had a sense of humor and a good imagination.

Spreading the blanket, he said, "Madam, our table awaits."

She giggled and sank down. "This is the steakhouse you were talking about?"

Sitting beside her, he gazed into her laughing hazel eyes and felt his body warm, even out in the cold. "Where are the cookies?"

She reached into her pocket and handed them to him.

He unwrapped the cloth. "Now, look out into that pasture. Do you see all those steaks on the hoof out there?"

Shaking her head, she laughed. "You are such a screwball."

"Maybe I am, but this here is the fanciest steakhouse you'll ever dine in. Naturally lit by God's own lighting, the moon and the stars, the finest beef in all the land and the best company you'll ever experience." Handing her a cookie, he said seriously, "Madam, it's advised that the beef just melts in your mouth."

He was doing everything he could to make her feel better and still she seemed down. He wasn't angry or upset even that she had burned their supper. She was trying, really trying to learn to be a cook. He couldn't fault her when things went wrong.

A shiver rattled through her. It was cold, yet it was also beautiful and quiet, and there was no lingering smell of burnt vegetables.

He wrapped his arm around her. "Let's snuggle to keep warm."

"How's your steak?" she asked.

"Hmmm. Delicious. Best cut of meat I've ever tasted. How about you, Mrs. Fraser, how is your steak?"

"I've never tasted anything better."

Smiling, he felt better, holding her in his arms as they finished off the last of the cookies.

"See, I told you this was a fine steakhouse."

When the cookies were all gone, he reached over and licked her bottom lip with his tongue. With his mouth almost touching hers, he said, "You had a crumb on your lip."

"Oh," she whispered as his mouth covered hers.

He moved his lips softly over hers, caressing her, doing his best to make her feel cherished and special.

Ethan knew that in order for Beth to be happy on the ranch, she had to feel like she was a part of this family operation. She needed to belong, and until she could accomplish some of the tasks given to her, she would never think this was where she was meant to live. He wanted her to feel like this was her home, their home, where the two of them would live forever.

His hands wrapped around her face, holding her in place, as he poured his feelings into his kiss. If given the chance, he wanted to worship her body. Gently, he pulled her down until she was lying flat on the blanket, while his lips never left hers. If given the chance, tonight he would take their marriage to the next step. It was past time, and he'd been patient.

Suddenly, she put a hand between them, pushing him back. He stopped and gazed at her, knowing she wasn't ready. He lay back on the roof, his breathing heavy, and gazed up at the stars. "I don't know what's holding you back."

She sighed. "I don't know either. Perhaps fear. Uncertainty. What if this isn't right for either of us?"

The only doubt in his mind was whether or not his rich wife would ever adjust to their life here on the ranch. That thought frightened him.

She shivered.

"Are you cold?"

"A little," she said.

Pulling her into his arms, they lay on top of the shed on a cold winter's night in the middle of a pasture with the cows braying. "This is nice."

"Yes, it is," she said. "The stars are not this bright in Chicago, and if the wind was blowing across the lake, you wouldn't want to be outside like this."

"Do you miss Chicago?"

"Some things, but not everything."

He laughed. "Yeah, I would miss some things about the ranch, but not everything."

"What are we going to do?" she asked softly.

Squeezing her tightly, he tried to relieve her fears. Only when she trusted and felt comfortable with him would she agree to consummate their marriage. He had to make her feel worshiped and wanted and somehow needed. "We're going to lay here until we get too cold. Then we're going to go inside and go to bed."

How many men would wait this long for their wedding night? How many men would have been this patient with her? And how could he continue like this? Sighing, he knew he had to be more patient and wait until his wife was ready, but it was getting damn hard.

"You know, I love being outdoors like this. When we build our house, I think we should have a place on the roof where we can go, when the children are asleep, where we can crawl up and look at the stars like this. Just you and me."

"That sounds lovely," she said. "But will they let us build a house?"

"That's the question." Frustration with his brothers filled him. "Of course, if you keep cooking like you did tonight, we may not have much choice."

"Ethan," she said outraged. "And here I was having such lovely thoughts about our place."

He reached down and kissed her lightly on the mouth. "Keep thinking them. Your cooking will improve, and soon you'll be making us dinner every night. And soon, very soon, we're going to conquer your fears and check out the bounce in our bed."

Turning to gaze at him, there was a mixture of shock and fear in her eyes and even a trace of what looked like desire. He had no doubts she wanted him. He had to continue to be patient with her.

"It's the truth, Mrs. Fraser." His mouth covered hers. His lips covering—

"Ethan," a man yelled. "Ethan, you out there?"

With a sigh, he moved away from her. "I'm here."

"What in tarnation are you doing up there?" Spunky asked.

"If I wanted you to know, I'd tell you," Ethan replied.

"Well, your mother is looking for you. She got worried and sent me out to find you. She wants to talk to you," Spunky said.

"Wonderful," he said sarcastically. "Tell her I'm busy right now. I'll come see her when I have time."

"Okay," he said, stretching his neck and peering up on the roof.

Just what Ethan didn't want or need at this moment, a chance to spend time with his mother. Yet again, maybe he should put more pressure on her about how they needed a house. Because soon, very soon, he hoped his wife would be expecting a child. His child.

"You up there with someone?"

"Yes, my wife."

"Oh—"

"Goodnight, Spunky," Ethan replied.

"Yeah, I'd say it was a good night."

"Ethan, you should go to your mother," Beth said quietly.

"Why? I'm enjoying time with my wife. Mother needs to learn that not everything happens in her time."

Beth giggled.

"What's so funny?"

"You are so much like your mother."

"Now those are fighting words, woman."

"Well, it's true."

"When our children are grown, please don't let me make decisions for them."

She reached up and touched his cheek. "I won't.

~

Ethan escorted Beth back into the barn and took his time walking across to the big house to see what his mother needed. It was getting late. What could she be wanting at this hour of the night?

Walking in, he found her rocking and knitting in front of an open fire. "Have a seat, son."

"I hope this is important," Ethan said. "I was busy."

She ignored his comment, which further frustrated him. What if he'd been making love to his wife?

"Your brother Jamie came to me and said you're wanting to build a house for you and Beth," she said.

"Yes," Ethan replied suddenly interested to hear what his mother had to say and if she would take his side. "I was going to wait until the family had their financial meeting and ask at that time that we build a home for my family."

She sighed. "Son, with me paying for the wives, I've stretched our budget kind of thin this year."

Ethan shook his head, fury roaring through him at the outrage. Had his mother even thought about what would be needed when they were all married and expecting children? Did she have a plan for more mouths to feed and house and clothe? Obviously not. "Did you ever think about where all of us would live after you married us off?"

"Of course I did."

"Then what's the problem? My wife wants a home, a place that has a parlor and bedrooms and a kitchen of her own."

"Your wife doesn't even know how to cook."

While what she said was true, Ethan felt duty bound to protect her from everyone, including his mother.

"That may be so, but she's learning, and eventually, she's going to know how. Where do you think our children will be born? In a barn? In a manger? I think that one has already been done."

His mother glared at him. "There is no need for you to be impertinent with me, young man."

"Excuse me, you're the one who insisted we all marry."

"And like a child, you're still mad about me finding you a woman. If you didn't want to get married, you should have said no. You're so busy claiming to be your own man, then stand up and be one."

He took a deep breath to stop the hateful things that were racing through his mind from reaching his mouth. This was his mother, and she deserved respect, even when he felt like she hadn't been respectful to him. Still, anger surged through his body, and it was all he could do to control what he wanted to say.

He jumped up from his chair. "All right. I'm standing up and being a man. I want a home for my wife, this year."

Sighing, his mother shook her head. "You really try me sometime."

"Same here."

"You're just like your father."

"No, I'm more like you," he said, recognizing Beth was right. They both were headstrong people who spoke their minds when pushed to their limits.

"Either way, why are you the one who fights me at every turn?" she asked.

There were so many reasons, but most of all she still thought of him as a ten-year-old boy she could boss around to do what she wanted him to do. But that had to stop. No longer would he take orders from his mother, unless he agreed with her. "Because you interfere, and I'm no longer putting up with it."

His mother puffed up like yeast in a loaf of bread. "I do not interfere. I simply make certain my children are all going in the right direction."

He almost laughed. She wanted all her children going in one direction? Did she think they were a herd, and she could just round them up and lead them in the direction she decided on?

"Well, leave me alone, or we'll be going in opposite directions."

"Ethan Daniel Fraser."

It was late, he was tired, and he'd put up with all the women he could handle for one day. First, his wife and now, his mother. Maybe Caleb had been right to want to remain single.

"I'm serious, Mother. Help convince everyone that we need a house, since you're the one who thought I needed a wife."

She shook her head. "Your older brother thinks we should wait at least another year."

Why were they being so strict with him? Why didn't they want to help him make this marriage last? Did they really think Beth would be happy living in a loft? He dared any of his brothers to move there with their wives and see just how long they'd last.

"My older brother's family has a home. Caleb has a home and Gideon has the parsonage."

"I'm not agreeing to help you."

"Then don't be surprised if Beth and I move to Chicago," he said and walked out the door.

It was an empty threat. He didn't want to leave the ranch, but his mother needed shaking up. Hopefully, he'd done just that.

~

The next evening, Ethan, frustrated that his family was resisting building them a house and his beautiful wife had yet to share his bed, disappeared into his woodworking shop at the back of the barn. Whenever he felt troubled, this was where he went to keep his hands busy and his mind occupied.

Picking up a fresh piece of wood, he rapidly marked and cut it.

He'd been working an hour when the door opened, and Beth walked in. "There you are. I've been looking for you."

"Is there something you need?"

"No, I just couldn't find you," she said, coming to stand behind him. "What are you doing?"

"Working on creating a frame," he said quietly. He'd gone to the barn to escape his frustrations. Yet, here he was beginning a rocker he hoped he would one day see her rocking their babies in.

"Oh, what will you do with it?" she asked.

"I don't know," he said lying. He wanted it to be a surprise and would give it to her when she was expecting his baby, if that ever happened. If not, surely one of his sisters-in-law could use it for their children.

"What are you doing now?"

"Making the wood smooth," he said, rubbing the roughened plank with the planer. As he worked, he became overheated in the workshop and removed his shirt.

She ran her fingers across the grain in the board. "It's smooth, so why are you still working on it?"

"I'm going to make the board curve," he said continuing. He could feel her eyes on his naked chest. Glancing up, he gazed at her, still moving the planer across the lumber.

"Can I try it?" she asked.

Shocked that his high-society wife was going to do woodworking with him, he moved over on the bench to make room for her. In the days they'd been married, she'd changed and grown.

"You'll get wood shavings on you."

"Can't be any worse than the mud I already have on me," she said.

"All right," he replied, glad she was going to be close to him. "Come sit in front of me."

She sat down on his workbench, and he wrapped his arms around her. Taking a deep breath, he decided her hair smelled like fresh rainwater.

She fit perfectly up against his chest, and it was all he could do not to nuzzle her neck and shoulders with his lips.

"What do I do?" she asked.

He placed her hands on the ripping chisel and laid his hands on top of hers. Together, they stripped the wood, his hands pushing hers as the wood shavings slid from the lumber. If he had his way, he would lay her down right here in his workshop and kiss her until they were both tearing at each other's clothes. But would she respond that way? He caught glimpses of passion in her eyes, but he didn't know if she was ready for them to be a true married couple.

She glanced back at him, her hazel eyes sparkling. "This is hard work, but look, the wood it's changing right before our eyes."

"Yes," he said, placing his head against hers, molding her to him. He felt the rate of her breathing increase, her lungs expanding.

"Surely you have some idea what you're going to make," she said, turning toward him.

Of course he did, but he wasn't going to tell her what the wood was for. In the future, it could be harder to keep it from her, but he truly hoped he would be able to surprise her.

He shrugged. "Maybe." Stopping, he took her hand and ran it across the wood, the way he wanted her to caress him. He was getting hard just thinking about her hands stroking his body. "Is it smooth?"

"Yes," she said breathlessly. "But I felt a bump."

He picked up a rag and wiped the wood clean. Then he ran his hand across the surface. Turning to her, he leaned against her face. "Now, we begin again."

Placing his hands over hers, they worked the chisel over the wood, smoothing it, until she pulled her hands free. He stopped and she turned to him, her breathing harsh, her eyes dilated, and he wanted to stop and carry her upstairs, but he didn't.

"Why do you do this?"

"Because I enjoy turning a piece of wood into something I can either use or give away. I like taking something that was the trunk of a tree and making a piece of furniture out of it."

"Oh," she said, gazing up at him. "I guess it's kind of like needlepoint or crochet."

"Yes," he said. "Do you do needlepoint?"

"Sometimes," she confessed. "Living here has given me a new appreciation for what it takes to run a household.

Before, I never saw what went on behind the prepared meals, the clean clothes, and the tidy house. Now I know."

Nodding, he tilted his head over her shoulder. "Not many people lead the kind of life you grew up with."

"I guess not," she said. "I never realized what money really afforded me until it was gone."

He knew her father was a banker, and Ethan would never in this lifetime make the kind of money her father made. Would she be happy living a simple life as a rancher's wife? God, how he hoped so because it would be hard to watch her walk away and leave him.

"Do you miss it?" he asked, his mouth close to her ear. She shivered.

"I miss things being taken care of for me. I don't miss the social aspect."

Stunned, he looked at her. "I thought that was what you would miss most."

She shook her head. "No. Women can be very catty, and I got tired of the games. I got tired of the *who is the perfect match* game, of everyone trying to find me a rich husband who fit my status in society."

"What about your family? Do you miss your father?"

She was silent for a long moment. "I was never very important to my father. I was more like a commodity he was trading than his daughter. I'm sure he's not missed me since I've been gone."

Her existence in Chicago sounded cold, yet there were times he felt like she had no intention of staying on the ranch. He had to convince her this was her home. Here with him was where she belonged.

"I'm glad you're here," he whispered softly against her ear again, his arms on either side of her.

"Thanks," she said, but she didn't say she was glad to be here. She didn't make any other remark than thanks, and that worried him.

"Anyway, I wanted to check on you."

Swinging her legs around, he pulled her onto his lap. "I'm fine, Mrs. Fraser." He leaned in and covered her mouth with his. His kiss was filled with promise, and longing, and forever, if that was what she wanted. Putting his hand behind her head, he held her mouth to his and kissed her like he could give her everything she wanted.

He pushed his tongue into her mouth, and she returned his caress as she sighed into his kiss. Moving his hand, he touched her breast with his hand, caressing her mound through her dress, needing to feel more of her, wanting to carry her upstairs and truly experience his wife.

Sliding his hand up her skirt, he slipped his fingers inside her pantaloons. Still not protesting, she allowed him to touch her womanly folds, and he felt the desire she'd managed to hide from him.

Abruptly, she pulled away, her eyes wide, her breathing harsh sounding. "I've got to go upstairs." After jumping up from the bench, she hurried out of the room. Then he heard her running up the steps.

Sighing, he tried to release the sexual frustration he could feel roiling inside him. He'd not gotten into his wife's bed, but at least he'd gotten into her pantaloons, and he knew she wanted him as much as he desired her.

They were closer.

Chapter Eight

Late the next afternoon, Beth had had all the mending and women's talk she could handle. She had to escape out into the bright sunshine and get away from the women chatting how wonderful their married lives were. She didn't believe it for an instant. They were just trying to one-up each other, and she'd reached her breaking point, so she left.

As she crossed the path between the house and the barn, the sun shone brightly, and Beth hoped this meant the snow would soon melt, and they would be able to travel into town. Gideon and Ruby were leaving in the morning by horseback, but the men said the snow was still too deep to get the wagon to town.

After Beth's earlier experience, she feared riding into Angel Springs by herself. So she waited, knowing each day was harder than the one before when Ethan kissed her. Since the day of their wedding, a tension had been growing between them that left her wanting more from Ethan. And she realized that the consummation of their marriage was getting harder and harder to resist.

She enjoyed how her body had responded with the feel of his mouth on hers, his tongue caressing her in ways she'd never dreamed of. Last night when he'd touched her, she'd never felt anything like that before. She should feel shame, but instead, that single caress had left her craving more of his touch.

Was this what happened between a man and a woman? She didn't know.

She'd all but run out of the woodworking room, knowing they would soon be man and wife in the perfect sense if she didn't get away.

The memory left her feeling hot and flushed, and gosh, her husband was more man than anyone she'd met in Chicago. If only she could convince him to return with her, they could live such a great life. But Ethan was a man's man. She knew without asking he wanted to remain here with his brothers, and the ranch he loved. And what would he do in Chicago? He hardly seemed the type to manage a bank.

As she neared the pigpen, she heard the animals grunting and shuffling about. They were such disgusting creatures, and of all the farm animals, they were the ones she disliked the most. There was just something about their greedy eyes and their slimy stout bodies that sent a shiver down her spine.

"Help! Help!"

Running, Beth saw Cat inside the pigpen surrounded by the burly pigs. "Cat Fraser, get out of there!" she screamed.

The little girl tried to get out of the slop, but a big black had Cat's clothing in his teeth. The mother sow saw her and squealed in alarm. The other pigs started hurrying as fast as their short little legs could move their heavy bodies. One of them banged into the little girl, and she screamed.

Without thinking, Beth hurled herself over the fence and dropped into the disgusting pen. She kicked the boar, trying to get him away from the little girl, but the pig refused to budge. Seeing the fright in Cat's eyes, Beth tried to draw the pig's attention away from the child. Finally, in desperation, she reached into the trough and threw feed at the animal. He released the child and turned his focus to Beth as did the other pigs.

Trudging through the muck, the animals hurried after Beth. Her skirt was slowing her down as it dragged through the sludge. How could this dress ever be the same? Or be clean again?

Almost to the fence, she felt a pig hit the back of her legs. Her stomach clenched as fear roared through, and she went sprawling into the muck, landing on her face. Knowing she had to get up or be trampled, she scrambled to her knees.

Jumping up, she reached Cat and picked up the little girl, running for the fence. The women in the house ran to the pen, with Mrs. Fraser screaming. Olivia reached them first, just as the men rode up in the yard.

"Give her to me." Olivia took Cat from Beth.

Ethan leaped over the fence, with a pole in his hand. "Get out while I push them back." He commanded

Mrs. Fraser helped her climb over the fence, while Ethan held the animals back with the wooden pole.

"What the hell happened? You don't go in the pigpen!" Ethan yelled at Beth.

Cat clung to Olivia. "He was gonna eat me. He tried to eat me just like Papa said."

"Oh, precious girl, you could have been killed. Papa told you not to go there." Olivia scolded the child.

Cat sighed. "I only wanted to touch their funny noses."

Ethan froze, and Beth could see the anger slowly draining from him. He'd thought she'd deliberately gone into that pigsty? Not a chance on your life would she ever enter that pen unless someone was in danger. Someone like Cat.

Beth's hands shook, just looking at that huge pig, had her knees knocking, her breath coming in little gasps.

Jamie came running up. "What's wrong?"

"Cat went into the pigpen and Beth pulled her out," Ethan said, removing his hat and running his hand through his hair. The worry and anger obviously tightly coiled within him.

Jamie stared at his daughter. "Cat, you know you're not supposed to play around the pigpen."

Olivia wiped her hands on her dress. "Thank heaven Beth needed fresh air and saw her."

His exasperation with his daughter showed in his stern frown at the little girl. Beth could see the fear that filled his eyes.

"You and Beth both could have been badly hurt." He released a deep sigh, shook his head, and glanced at Beth. "Thank you."

Beth nodded. Her teeth were chattering and she felt numb. Cold was beginning to seep through her dress, permeating her pantaloons. The smell, a horrible stench that had the men taking a step back from her, assaulted her nose. How could she blame them? She too wanted to escape the smell that wafted from her clothing.

Was this typical of the way life on the ranch was lived? One simple accident could put you six feet under? A wild animal, an avalanche, or a forest fire could kill you in a second. How did people live like this every day?

"I'm going to get Beth into the loft. She's not looking so good," Ethan said.

"Come on, Cat. You've caused enough trouble for one day," Jamie said to his daughter.

"Tell the men I'll see them tomorrow." Ethan wrapped his arm around Beth, leading her away.

"You…don't…have…to do…this," she said between shakes. "I'm…okay."

"The hell you are. You're shaking like you lost nine lives today. You were so brave, Beth."

"No…I couldn't…get to her…fast enough."

"You saved her," Ethan responded. "I'd hug you, but you're pretty stinky."

She shook her head at him, unable to talk she was so cold.

As they walked into the barn, he stopped. "Sorry, honey, but I think this dress would be better left here."

What could she say? She could smell the stench on her and knew this odor would forever be associated with pigs and her escapade in the pen.

She reached behind her, and he shooed her hands away. "Let me."

Methodically, he undid the buttons on the back of her dress then peeled the soggy, stinky garment from her body. Standing in the barn in just her chemise, petticoats, and pantaloons, her shivers seemed to double. The realization of what she'd done caused her body to shake from nerves, and the cold held her its grip.

"I think it would be best if you took a bath."

Nodding, she knew he would see her naked, yet she didn't have the strength to fight him. She wasn't even sure she wanted to. They were married, he was her husband, and she'd almost died in that pen this afternoon.

"Honey, you stink."

"Thanks," she said. "Lots of hot water, please."

"Let's get you upstairs. Don't want one of the hands coming into the barn and finding you in your drawers." He helped her to the loft, but when they reached the door, he stopped. "Stay put. I'm going to heat some water. Then I'll help you remove the rest of your clothes out here, so we keep the stink out of our home." He softened his words with a grin.

He hurried through the door, and all she could think about was what a fine day this had turned into. After last night, she feared that if Ethan saw her naked, there could possibly be fireworks, and it wasn't even the fourth of July.

When he returned, he laid a towel down then slipped her petticoats from her waist. Next went her chemise. She brought her hands up to cover her breasts, but he didn't even pay her any mind. He slowly removed her pantaloons, dropping the last garment onto the towel. Wrapping a blanket around her, he led her into the loft.

She was cold, she was numb, she was frightened, yet this man was gently taking care of her, and she knew that couldn't be pleasant. A giggle came from her lips as she thought of the society girls.

"What's so funny?" he asked.

"I had a random thought about the girls back home. I couldn't help but wonder what they would think of me now," she said laughing. "Oh Miss Worthington, you're perfume is quite atrocious."

He squeezed her arm. "But it's Mrs. Fraser now, and what you don't realize is you saved Cat's life. Those pigs could have trampled that child. So Mrs. Fraser, I don't care what you smell like. You're my wife."

The words were simple, yet they were said with such pride a warm feeling gathered in her stomach. "I was so scared, Ethan."

"But you didn't let that fear stop you. You saved her, Beth. I'm so proud of you."

A tear trickled down her cheek, and he quickly swiped it away. "No need to cry, honey. You're safe. Cat's safe. And soon you'll be warm and smell quite delicious again."

She laughed. "I don't smell good right now?"

"I love your scent, but not so much the pigs."

He poured the first bucket of hot water into the tub. Then he added some cooler water. Quickly, he put more water on the stove to warm again. "Sorry it's taking so long."

Now she appreciated all the effort her staff at home had given to make certain she had a nice hot bath waiting for her. Never again would she take them for granted.

"That's okay," she said. "I think I'll get in."

When she stepped toward the tub, he put his hand beneath her elbow to steady her. "Close your eyes," she said.

"Sure," he answered.

She dropped the blanket, past the point of caring, needing the hot water to cleanse her, warm her, and make her feel better.

"But I'm peeking."

"Ethan!" she cried.

"You're my wife. We're joined as one," he whispered. "And frankly, I like what I see."

She didn't have the energy to argue with him. She was tired. She'd been terrified, so afraid Cat that precious little girl was going to get killed right in front of Beth's eyes.

She sank into the warm water. "I can't fight anymore."

"Oh, I don't want to fight you," he whispered as he picked up a wet washcloth and wiped her face clean. "Let me bathe you."

He pushed her down into the tub, getting her hair wet. She sighed when she felt his fingers running through her hair, and she realized he was washing it for her. "I could do that."

"No, let me take care of you," he said softly.

Nothing had ever felt so good, so right. Her husband was washing her hair, and she'd never even considered he would ever want to bathe her. He was taking care of her, and while she knew he shouldn't be seeing her naked, no one since her mother had ever taken care of her like this. She felt almost worshiped.

Pouring warm water over her head, he rinsed her then took the washcloth and quickly bathed her.

"You shouldn't," she weakly protested.

"And why not?"

"Because I'm not a child." But how could she refuse him when he was being so kind, so good to her? He was making certain she was getting warm and clean.

"Some day you can repay the favor when I get injured," he said. "This is what a man and wife do for one another. They take care of each other."

Thinking back to her parents' marriage, she couldn't come up with any memories of a loving couple, just two people who'd shared the same house, the same space. If there had been warmth in their marriage, it had only occurred behind closed doors.

"Stand," he said, helping her to her feet.

Slowly, he poured hot water over her, rinsing her naked body. When the pail was empty, he picked up a towel he'd laid nearby. Starting at her head, he towel dried her hair as best he could. Then he moved down her body. The feel of his hands through the towel rubbing her wet skin had her shivering again but not from cold this time. No, she was shivering from the warmth permeating every cell, radiating, creating feelings she'd never experienced.

He wrapped the towel around her. "Sit on the bed and let me comb your hair."

She watched as he found her comb and began to detangle her long tresses.

"You have beautiful hair."

"Thank you."

"I've watched you brushing it at night before you go to bed, and it looks so soft."

She swallowed, trying to keep this feeling, this urge she'd never felt before, from consuming her. Finally, he finished and she thought he was done with her.

"Crawl up under the covers. You'll stay warm." He began to remove his clothes. "We're going to spend the evening together."

A trickle of anticipation and fear spiraled through her. Was he saying what she thought he meant? Did she dare ask? He didn't stop when he removed his pants. Oh no, he went right down to bare skin, and as much as she wanted to look away, she couldn't. Her husband was rock solid gorgeous. His flat stomach and abs rippled with muscle, and his strong chest supported his massive arms. Her eyes roamed down to his manhood, and her lungs froze. His member was sticking out, just as hard and muscled as the rest of the man.

They were husband and wife, and in that moment she knew there would be no saying *no* tonight. And she didn't want to. She'd almost died today. Tonight she wanted to live in her husband's arms.

~

Ethan had been a patient man. He'd given her time. He'd waited until they were comfortable with each other. He'd courted her, he'd comforted her, and now he'd taken care of her. Beth was his wife, and the time had come for them to become husband and wife in every sense of the word, including lying together.

Crawling into the bed beside her naked, he pulled her into his arms. "Cold?"

"No, not any longer," she whispered. "Thank you."

He smiled at her, his heart filled with happiness. He was lying in bed with his wife. "You're welcome, Mrs. Fraser. I told you I'd be a good husband to you."

"And you are."

"Not to mention, you smell like my Beth again."

Her full womanly body felt like heaven melded against him. There was no other place he wanted to be right now but here beside his wife, taking care of her, making sure she felt safe and secure in his arms.

She reached up and caressed the side of his face, her hazel eyes wide with wonder. "You know how I smell?"

"I do and it's very intoxicating," he said, kissing her cheek, his lips trailing down to her ear, where he traced the outer edge with his tongue. "You taste good too."

"Ethan," she said with a sigh.

"Yes, Beth," he replied, his voice a soft whisper caressing her ear. He continued, his lips moving down her neck, leaving soft breathy kisses, his tongue trailing along her skin. When he reached the bottom of her neck, she arched her back, her breathing heavy.

God, he hoped she didn't ask him to stop because he would slowly die of frustration if he didn't get to bed his wife tonight.

He rolled her onto her stomach and continued moving his mouth down her back, his hands gently massaging her muscles. She shuddered beneath his touch, her flesh trembling.

"Do you want me to stop?"

"Oh God, no," she whispered. "This feels so good."

Smiling, he continued until he reached her buttocks and gently bit her sweet, heart-shaped derriere.

"Ouch!"

"Sorry, it was just too tempting. You have such a beautiful backside, Mrs. Fraser." He kissed the tender spot then returned the same way he'd come, but this time he halted at the back of her neck, letting his tongue trail over the most vulnerable area.

"Oh, Ethan," she cried. "What are you doing?"

"I'm kissing you," he whispered against her neck. Rolling her over, he stared into her hazel eyes filled with passion. "Oh Beth, I've waited so long for us to be together."

He lowered his lips to hers, claiming her, making her his. Slanting his mouth over hers, he kissed her, knowing he could have lost her today, knowing this was a second chance. They had been given a new opportunity to begin their marriage, and he was going to do that right now.

No more waiting. Tonight would be a night they would never forget because he would make her his woman, his lover, his wife.

With his mouth, he stroked her tender lips until she was whimpering for him. Urgent and hungry for her, he plundered her mouth, devouring her with the fierceness of his desire. Greed to be with his wife and claim her as his own filled him.

Surrounded by the scent of his sweet Beth, he trailed his fingers down the soft skin of her shoulders to her breasts. Those sweet luscious melons she'd tried so hard to hide and he'd ached with fervor to touch.

She ran her hands down his shoulders and across his back, urging him on as he broke the kiss and moved his mouth to taste her creamy white breasts. Her pink nipples lay puckered in a rosy shadow. The touch of her hands against his back, massaging and coaxing and urging him on, encouraged him to brush his lips against the furrowed kernel of her nipple. His tongue circled her areola, giving her pleasure as he suckled his wife's breasts.

"Ethan," she cried, arching into his mouth, giving him even more access. This woman excited him beyond his wildest dreams. He wanted to make her first time special. He wanted to give her more than she deserved, to show her that being with her husband was wonderful and full of pleasure.

His hand skimmed down her stomach, reaching her moist woman center. Sliding his fingers into her, he gently massaged the velvety folds, eliciting a moan from between her lips. As she clung to him, he coaxed her intimately.

What was it about her that made him want to protect her? He felt like she had no one. No one but him, and he wanted to make sure he gave her his best because she deserved it, and more.

In all his years of growing up and becoming a man, he'd never dreamed of feeling this way toward a woman, but now he knew how his father had felt about his mother, how he'd desired to give her the world, even when he could only afford a small piece of Colorado. Ethan wanted to make certain his Beth received the very best he could give her. He would protect her and shelter her from the storms of life the best he could.

Her hands fisted in the sheets, her hair splayed across his pillow. Suddenly her body tensed around him, and she lifted up, arching her back as she cried out, "Ethan!"

His blood pounded with the primitive need to possess her. Eagerly, he rose over her. Parting her legs, he hesitated at the entrance to her. As he gazed down at her as dusk settled over the room, she had never looked more beautiful than she did at this moment.

Her breathing was labored, her flesh wet and quivering with need for him. His lips covered hers once more in a kiss that joined them as he slowly pushed into her, meeting the resistance of her maidenhead. With a final shove, he went forward, and she broke the kiss, crying out.

"It's okay. Take a deep breath and soon it'll feel better."

She gazed at him, her eyes filled with trust, her bottom lip quivering. "I'm okay."

Slowly, he moved within her tight body. He so wanted to bury himself deeply within her sweet folds, but he held back, waiting, letting her adjust to him. Her hips began to move slowly at first, but then with more confidence, as she stared at him, her passion filling the empty corners of his soul.

"That's it, Beth," he encouraged her.

"Oh, Ethan, this feels wonderful," she whispered as her eyes expressed the unspoken words between them. This connection they'd forged tonight could last them a lifetime.

He moved her hands up by her head and gripped them, pushing into her as she met his thrusts. With the rock of her hips, he plunged into her sweetness, knowing that with each pounding thrust she seeped into his soul and his heart. Deep, resonant pleasure emitted from each long, slow stroke and swirled him closer and closer to the edge. He longed to slow rising tide of delight hurtling him faster and faster toward the shore, but he could no more stop than quit breathing.

Soon, they were plunging headfirst over the cliff together, her cry of satisfaction imprinting on his heart.

Spent, he rolled to his side, pulling her against him, needing to feel her softness surrounding him.

He'd never expected to experience this kind of gratification with his wife, the woman he barely knew who'd been thrust into his life, and now he could never imagine living without her.

How had Beth captured his soul so quickly?

~

Beth woke early the next morning before it was time to get up. She lay next to her husband and thought about what had happened the night before.

They'd made love. The words reverberated through her brain as she felt Ethan's warm body curled around her. He was so handsome and strong, and muscular and manly, and poor.

She swallowed. It wasn't about the money. Really, it wasn't, and no, he wasn't living in poverty by any means. The ranch was obviously a successful family operation, but compared to the wealth of her father and his cronies, they weren't rich. Yet in so many ways, they led happier, healthier lives. No, there were no big fancy parties, rubbing noses with the elite in town, or at least, there hadn't been yet.

But the plan all along had been to marry, get a copy of the wedding license, and catch the next train back to Chicago, where she would return to her everyday life a rich young woman who never had to marry.

Why did that life sound so cold after experiencing the Fraser family? Clearly, she'd been the outsider, but there was warmth and a sense of caring here, even when they were upset at one another. And once she was able to show them her worth and value, they would gladly open their arms to her.

But still, the original plan had been to marry then return to Chicago before she had sex with her husband. And now, she'd consummated the marriage, making it impossible to annul if she ever wanted to remarry.

Glancing at her husband, she felt the incredible urge to wipe the dark hair away from his face. He'd been so caring last night, so gentle, bathing and washing her, she'd felt incredibly spoiled. And when he'd made love to her…she'd never experienced anything so wonderful. But they couldn't do it again, or she could find herself pregnant. Then she'd have no choice but to remain here in the middle of nowhere.

He stirred, his arms tightening around her like he was afraid she'd get away. Suddenly, he tensed. "You awake?"

"Yes," she said softly. "I think these early hours are growing on me."

Laughing, he kissed her cheek. "We better get up and make a showing this morning. Everyone will be worried about you."

"I have a problem," she said, sitting up and holding the blanket in front of her. "I don't have anything to wear."

The hated dress had finally met its death in the pigpen, for there was no way she would ever wear that rag again. The memories were just too fresh, too frightening.

"Not a problem as far as I can see," he said grinning. "I kind of like you naked."

She shook her head at him. "I don't think your sisters-in-law or your mother would approve of me running around without clothes in front of your brothers."

"Well, for that matter, neither would I. But here in the loft, oh honey, please don't get dressed on my account."

She could feel the blush rise up on her cheeks. The man was incorrigible, yet just gazing at him she felt her body start to warm all over again.

"Ethan," she said sternly. "My dress is in the barn full of pig manure."

"That *is* a problem," he admitted.

He rose, walked over to his clothes, and pulled on his pants. She wanted to call him back to bed and say "No, don't go yet." Last night had been more than she'd ever dreamed of when she'd thought of what happened between a man and a woman. Last night had been simply glorious.

"Give me a few minutes and I'll see what I can do."

As he slipped on his shirt, she kind of regretted him covering up that fabulous chest and those muscles.

He glanced back at her then came to the bed. Leaning down, he kissed her full on the mouth. "Good morning, Mrs. Fraser. Last night was the best."

She blushed and couldn't help but think he was right. "Is it always like that between two people?"

He grinned. "Nope. Not at all. We're lucky."

Rising up, he shoved his hat on his head. "I'll be back with some clothes for you."

Chapter Nine

The sun was just starting to lighten up the eastern sky, as Ethan walked across the frozen ground to the main house. He really didn't want to speak to his mother, but considering the circumstances, he had no choice. Knocking the snow off his boots, he opened the door and walked in.

She was sitting at her desk, still in her robe. "Is Beth okay?" She stood and walked toward him. "I wanted to come check but thought it was better you take care of her."

"Thank you. I did," he said, knowing how hard it must have been for his mother not to come over and interfere.

"And she's all right?"

"Yes, she's fine, but her clothes aren't. She doesn't have another dress."

His mother's brows rose in a questioning manner. She opened her mouth to say something then stopped herself. After taking a deep breath, she said, "Follow me. I'll see if I can find her something. She was the only one of the brides not to bring a trunk."

Ethan knew she badly wanted to know why, but he wasn't going to indulge her. Later, he would tell her, but for now, she needed to learn not to interfere.

They walked up the stairs to his mother's bedroom. She went to an armoire and opened it. Going through the clothes, she finally said, "Here's one she could wear. Does she need women's undergarments?"

"She needs everything."

His mother opened the dresser and pulled out some things. "These are going to be so big on her, but they'll work." She handed the stack of garments to him. "I'm so grateful she was there to rescue Cat. It was very brave of her to jump into that pen and pull the child out. We were lucky."

"Yes, I know. But I believe when something bad happens, sometimes a little bit of good comes out of it." He smiled.

She gazed at him oddly.

He turned away. "Thanks, Mother."

Hurrying back down the stairs, he couldn't keep the grin off his face. It was going to be a wonderful day and an even better night. He couldn't wait to get back home tonight and cuddle with his sweet wife.

As he opened the door, his eldest brother stepped into the house. "Morning, Ethan."

"Morning," he said, not feeling friendly toward Jamie just yet. Beth could be pregnant. They needed a home of their own before the little ones started to arrive, and he couldn't wait to see his wife's belly rounded with his child.

Jamie sighed. "I just want to say thank you again to Beth for saving Cat. I've buried a wife. I couldn't bear to lose a child."

Ethan nodded. "We were lucky yesterday no one got hurt."

"Yes," Jamie agreed.

"You know, Jamie, my wife could be pregnant right now. We could be expecting our first child, and I'm not raising children above that barn. If you want us to stay, then help me find a way to construct a home for my family."

"Ethan, I'd like nothing better, but we've got expenses and more mouths to feed, and we don't know what the spring is going to bring. If we have a good year, absolutely. If not, I can't risk the ranch to build a home for you and your bride."

Ethan sighed. He knew the money was there. He'd worked hard for the ranch and never expected much in return. But now, because his mother had found him a bride, he expected his brother and mother to find a way to build him a home.

He heard his mother come down the stairs and even glanced over at her, including her in the conversation. "I've never asked for anything before. But this time, I'm not giving in. If you want us to stay and not go off on our own, then you'll build us a home. Have a good day."

Ethan strode out the door. He had to get back to his bride.

~

As she worked her needle through Ethan's shirt, Beth glanced around the room at her sisters-in-law, Olivia and Lillian. Both women seemed to have adapted to their new homes and husbands. This afternoon Olivia had invited the women to her home to do their mending together.

Olivia seemed to enjoy taking care of the children, and she and Jamie appeared happy. Lillian had her hands full with her husband, Caleb, but even she seemed to be glowing.

"Do you ladies realize we've been here almost three weeks?" Olivia said. "It just doesn't seem possible."

"I wonder which one of us is going to come up with a child first?"

"I think all of us will soon have little ones to tend to besides me," Olivia said. "Right now, I have my hands full and don't need a baby, though a child of my own would be nice."

"What about you, Beth?" Lillian asked.

"I'm in no hurry," Beth answered, tying a knot in her thread. Fear raced through her at the idea of expecting a child. If she became pregnant, there was no way she could ever leave Ethan. And after last night, it was possible. Dear God, she could have just ruined everything.

There was silence for a few moments as they all worked on the mending of their husbands' shirts. It was a first for Beth. Sure, she knew how to use a needle, but she'd never mended anything in her life. And now here she was sewing buttons back onto his shirts.

"You know, I think Ruby was already in the family way when we arrived," Olivia said. "She confessed to me she was a widow."

"Can you imagine her husband died, then she found out she was pregnant? No man with a baby to raise? No wonder she became a mail-order bride. I just hope Gideon is good to her child."

"Oh, I think he'll accept that baby and love it like his own," Olivia responded.

Beth sat back and ran her needle through her husband's shirt. Holding it up close to her face, she breathed in her husband's essence. What was it about Ethan that just the smell of him had her remembering last night? She'd never dreamed it could be so good between a man and a woman. She couldn't imagine her mother and father being this close, yet she'd loved being in his arms, the feel of his naked body against hers.

"Oh Beth, come back…you've drifted off, hopefully somewhere really pleasant," Olivia teased.

"Sorry," she said, taking a deep breath and running another loop of thread through the wooden button.

"You and Ethan seem to be getting along nicely. Jamie told me he spotted the two of you up on that old shed the other night, kissing," Olivia said smiling.

"He was showing me the stars," Beth replied. She was not about to let these women know her marriage was nothing but a farce, and she would be catching the next train out of town. And after last night, she had to get out of here soon. No pregnancies for her. No babies.

"I bet that wasn't all he was showing you," Lillian said with a laugh. "Are you happy?"

"Oh, yes," Beth lied. Well, it wasn't an entire lie. Last night had been wonderful, but still it changed nothing. This was not the life for her, and she had no intentions of becoming a rancher's wife. She continued working on Ethan's shirt. "What about you, ladies? Are you happy?"

Olivia sighed. "This is certainly not what I expected, but Jamie is a lovely man."

"And Caleb certainly knows how to make a woman feel special," Lillian said, staring down at her husband's shirt, ripping it slightly as she held it so tight.

Olivia didn't look up from her mending. "I guess I never considered how married life would be with children never giving you time alone until bedtime."

Beth laughed. "Or how it would be just the two of you in that small loft area above the barn. I mean, we're always together, except during the day. Sometimes I think I'd like just ten minutes alone in that bed. Just ten minutes before he wraps around me."

"You'd be asleep by the time he crawled in, and then you couldn't…you know," Lillian said.

Olivia laughed. Then her face grew serious and her voice softer. "You've both been intimate with your husbands?"

Beth nodded, thankful she didn't have to lie after last night.

Lillian smiled and nodded.

"Good, I thought I was the only one who had. I figured the rest of you would wait a while." She quickly glanced down at her husband's shirt, not meeting the other women's eyes.

Something wasn't right. Beth didn't know exactly what, but it just felt like none of them were being honest, and that bugged her.

These women were nice. She really liked them, but if they couldn't be honest with one another, then why stick around? But then again, she wasn't being honest with Ethan or any of the family. She was just waiting on the roads to clear. Then she would be heading to town to buy her ticket home to Chicago.

Before she became pregnant and was forced to stay here and have Ethan's baby.

~

Late that evening, Ethan came up the stairs to the loft, wanting only to spend some time with Beth before he crawled in bed. He was tired, and tomorrow he had a long trip into town to pick up supplies for the ranch. The snow was just beginning to melt, and the road would be a sloppy mess. He wasn't looking forward to the trip. It would take hours to get there, and he'd be trying to make it back before dark, hoping another snowstorm didn't blow in on his way home.

When he walked in the door, Beth was on the sofa, reading one of his books. For just an instant, he couldn't believe he was so lucky. This beautiful woman was his wife. If this was just a dream, it was a really good one..

"Hi," she said, glancing up at him. "You look tired."

"I am," he replied, walking over to give her a quick kiss on the lips. He leaned back then forward to kiss her again, holding her mouth to his as his lips brushed over hers in a way that left him hungering for more. When he pulled away, he grinned at her. "That's a great way to come home every night."

She smiled. "I saved you some dinner if you're hungry."

"Thanks." He sank onto the sofa and pulled off his boots. Right now, he just wanted to relax. He leaned back against the sofa and breathed in the scent of his wife. "The roads have cleared enough. I'm going into town tomorrow."

"Great, I'll come with you," she said, shutting her book, her hazel eyes excited at the prospect. "I can do some shopping and pick up some things I'm needing. Maybe we can spend the night and go out to dinner. Of course, I'll have to have an appropriate dress to wear. I can get some work dresses and a nightgown. I really need a nightgown."

He stared at her, watching the excitement cross her face, and didn't know how to tell her. Times like this made him realize just where she came from and how much she probably missed the entertainment of living in a big city and how little the ranch and his world had to offer her. "You're not going to town with me tomorrow."

"Why not?"

"Because the road is too dangerous and if the wagon gets stuck, I don't want you stranded out in the snow with me," he said. "Wait, and we'll go soon."

"Soon! That's not definitive. No, I want to go with you tomorrow," she said, her eyes wide, flashing angrily in the light.

How quickly they'd gone from having a great time last night to fighting. He knew without touching her there was no way she was going to let him close to her tonight. She was getting madder by the second. And all because he was trying to protect her.

"Look, there's maybe one dress shop and a mercantile. There's really not that much in town. Wait and we'll go to Denver soon."

She huffed up fatter than a Christmas turkey. "There are womanly things I need. Things you don't know how to buy."

"Then make me a list."

"No, I need to pick them out," she said, standing and pacing with her hands on her waist.

There was no winning this argument. No matter what he offered it wouldn't be right. He might as well just accept his punishment because she was going to deal it out. "You'll have to wait. I'm only going because the ranch has a list of things we need, and I don't know when the next snowstorm will hit, possibly snowing us in for the winter."

She stuck out her bottom lip at him, and he realized they were having their first argument. She was acting like a spoiled child, and with clarity, he realized she really didn't think of anyone but herself. She had no idea that the space she took up in the sleigh meant something else was not coming back with him to the ranch. There was only so much he could load into the back or else the vehicle would get stuck in the mud, and he wasn't about to stop and dig it out every five minutes.

After sucking in a long breath, he sighed, got off the sofa, and walked to the stove to heat his supper. Maybe this would all blow over after she had a few minutes to think about his reasons. "There is not enough room in the sleigh for you to come with me. You'll make the load even heavier. That would be dangerous. When the road clears, then I'll take you to town, but not this trip."

"And when will the road clear? Spring?"

"No, just like when you were brought from town, eventually, we'll use the sleigh and not the wagon. Make a list of what's urgent, and I'll pick up those items for you."

She shook her head and walked away, her back rigid, and he knew she was mad. A few minutes later, she came out from behind the screen, wrapped up in the extra blanket. She pulled her pillow off the bed and lay down on the sofa.

So, they were back to her sleeping in another location. The next time his mother wanted him to get married, he had to remember how difficult getting along with a stubborn woman could be.

He'd come home exhausted, hoping to spend the night with his wife wrapped in his arms, and instead, he now had a cold, empty bed to himself.

Chapter Ten

Early the next morning, Beth rose before her husband and hurried outside the barn. She did her chores. Then with a determined stride, she scampered over to the wagon before Ethan came down from the loft. The man didn't know his wife if he thought he was going into town without her. In fact, she'd packed her little valise and was all ready to catch the train back to Chicago.

All she had to do now was sell the brooch, purchase the ticket, and she'd be on her way back to civilization. Part of her was excited, but part of her would miss Ethan. Her chest ached at the thought of never seeing him again, and she had to shake herself. She didn't belong here. Sure, his kisses moved her, and she would never forget the night they'd made love, but a ranch in the mountains of Colorado was no place for a socialite like herself. Mrs. Fraser, her sisters-in-law, their husbands, and the children, she would miss them all, but she'd send them a Christmas card or maybe even a gift.

Today, she'd catch the train to Chicago and put this all behind her.

Quickly, she located the worn wooden wagon that had brought her to the ranch parked outside the barn. Hopefully, this was what he would drive to town today. She climbed into the back of the wagon, slid underneath the wooden bench, and pulled a tarp she'd found over herself. Laying on the hard surface of the wood planks, she knew this was not going to be an enjoyable ride. It had been a jolting jaunt on the way out of town, and since the blizzard, the road couldn't be any better.

Hearing footsteps, she quickly buried herself beneath the tarp and remained still.

"Shh, boy," Ethan said.

She heard the clink of metal then the thunk of something slapping against a body and realized he was saddling a horse. In another moment, she heard him tightening the cinch.

"Here's the list of what we need," Jamie said, slapping it into Ethan's hand. "Be careful little brother and get back before dark."

"Thanks. Look out for Beth today. She was already busy when I awoke. I'm concerned about her."

"Why? What's wrong?"

"Oh, she's mad at me."

Jamie laughed. "Your first marital spat."

There was silence for a moment. Then Ethan said, "She wanted to go to town today."

"She has no idea how lucky she is not to have to ride in the wagon. I'll find her and see if I can get her involved with Olivia and the kids."

A warning tingle raced up Beth's spine, and she began to doubt her decision to hide in the back.

"Thanks. I guess I better get going."

With a lurch, the wagon started forward, and Beth grabbed hold of a side board, trying to keep from moving and sliding in the space. The wagon bounced along the trail, and she felt like her bones were being tested as she rattled and tried to remain quiet.

An hour dragged by, and she couldn't help but start to think she would be nothing but black and blue and frozen by the time this ride was over. It hadn't seemed so long when she'd ridden out with the other women. But then, they'd been bundled together, chatting away, eagerly anticipating arriving at their new home. At least the other women had been. Beth had been dreading meeting her new husband, yet now when she thought of him, warmth rippled through her. She'd stay hidden until they were in town.

Then she would slip off and buy her train ticket and ride out of town.

Even though it was the best solution for both of them, it felt wrong, but she had no choice. She needed to get back to Chicago, to the life she had left behind. Though compared to these people, it seemed such a shallow existence—endless parties, dresses, and gossip about who was wearing what and who was engaged to whom. In the scheme of life, was that really all there was?

But it was the life she knew. There were no dangerous pigpens or cows needing to be milked or goats or jobs for her to do. And now that she was no longer on the marriage market, what would her life in Chicago be like? Still, she wanted to go home.

Suddenly, the wagon hit something hard, and her body flew up into the air. Her head hit the seat above her. Then she slammed down onto the wooden cargo area.

"Ouch!" she screamed.

"What the hell?" Ethan said, and she felt the horses slowing.

Tarnation, he'd heard her scream and was pulling the wagon to a stop. They came to a halt, and the tarp was yanked from her hands. Lying there, she glanced up at her husband.

"Hi, honey," she said with a smile, hoping it would cool the anger she could see building on his face. He wasn't too happy to see her.

"I told you that you couldn't come today."

"I know, but I wanted to go and spend time with you. I was going to surprise you when we arrived in town."

"Beth, you don't understand. It's dangerous out here. I was trying to protect you." He reached into his pocket, pulled out his handkerchief, and touched the side of her head. "Come here," he said, tugging her up by her arm. "You hit your head on the seat and split it open."

"Ouch," she said as he tenderly touched her head and wiped away the blood.

"You should have listened and stayed home."

If he saw her valise, he would know she was leaving. Somehow, she had to distract him and keep his attention focused on her. "I'm sorry. I wanted to have some time with you, and I thought even if we didn't spend the night, we'd be alone together. I could do some shopping while you did your business."

Frowning, he helped her out of the back of the wagon. "You'll sit up beside me. If we weren't almost to town, I would turn back and take you home, but it's too late now."

She reached out and hugged him. "Thank you, Ethan." She gave him a quick kiss on the lips. His eyes warmed and changed color.

"I'm not trying to be mean to you, Beth. I want to look out for you. You don't know the mountains yet, and I fear for your safety."

No one had ever wanted to protect her before, and his words warmed her from the inside out. Ethan Fraser was a good man, a worthy man, and she was going to walk away from him.

"I know, Ethan, and I appreciate it. I just needed to get off the ranch for a while," she said.

"Winter has just begun. Wait until we're snowbound for a couple of months. Then you'll really feel the need to go to town," he said. "Come on. Let's get you up front, so we can get going."

He helped her into the seat then crawled up beside her. "And one more thing, Beth. Don't do this again. I don't want to find you frozen under the seat. If you disagree with my decision, we talk about it."

"All right," she said, thinking this would not be a problem. Hopefully by tonight, she'd be on a train back to Chicago with the mountains and Ethan behind her?.

~

An hour later they pulled into town, and Beth gazed at the dismally small village. It wasn't even big enough to be called a town or city. When the train pulled in that night weeks ago, they'd been hurried into the waiting sleigh and headed out to the ranch. Now in the daylight, she could see the two blocks of stores and shops and saloons, and Lord, have mercy, one city block in Chicago was bigger than this entire town.

"I told you it wasn't much," he said, glancing at her, his dark brown eyes sparkling with laughter.

It must have shown on her face, though she was doing her best to hide the disappointment. How could she have ever imagined living in a place like this? There was nothing here but a few churches, a mercantile, a dress shop, blacksmith, baker, and a saloon. One lonely restaurant offered service at the end of the block, sort of your last eatery before heading out of town.

"I don't remember much about the night we came into town. It was dark, though I remember hearing music. I thought there was a play," she said with a sigh.

Ethan chuckled. "No that's from Miss Hattie's, where whiskey is cheap and the women…" He stopped.

She raised her brows at him. "Yes?"

"Let's just end it with the women are not as beautiful as my wife," he said, grinning at her.

"You are certainly a charmer, Mr. Fraser. We've never discussed the other women in your life besides Alyssa. Were there others?"

"Riding into the town where everyone I ever courted lives is somehow not the time to discuss them."

Laughing, she spotted the train station not far from the mercantile. She'd have to hurry if she didn't want to get caught. There was so much to accomplish in order to sneak out of town.

Ethan glanced at his watch. "I was invited for a late lunch with Ruby and Gideon, and now you're coming with me. I'll drop you off, and you can shop for an hour. I'll run to the lumber store and the mercantile and pick you up at the women's boutique." He pulled the wagon to a halt, and she smiled and jumped out.

Grabbing her valise out of the back, she watched as he stared at her, a weird expression on his face.

"Why do you have your suitcase?"

"I thought I would bring in the garments I have and compare them with what I need."

His brows rose, and his hands steadied the reins. "I guess that's one way to bring your undies with you."

She started to walk off when he asked her, "Don't you need some money?"

She hadn't even considered she had very little cash on her. Before, she'd always had her dressmaker send the bill to her father. She'd expected to do the same here. She had a brooch Henry had given her, but to cash it in would mean she'd need to go to the mercantile, where she could bump into her husband. And she wanted to use her cash for her train ticket.

Pulling out his wallet, he handed her a wad of bills. "That should be enough to purchase you a new dress and the proper women's undergarments."

Leaning up, she kissed him on the cheek. "Thanks, Ethan." She hesitated, knowing this could be the last time she ever saw him, and she felt a lump rise in her throat.

"What?"

Shaking her head, she bit her lip. "I'm so glad I came with you." It wasn't a total lie. It did fit the situation, and she would miss his sweet face.

"You're a stubborn woman." Grinning, he lifted the reins, and soon, the wagon was rattling down Main Street.

She waited until he turned the corner then hurried as fast as her legs would carry her to the train station. She was free. She was getting away and returning home, yet it didn't feel right. Watching him turn the corner, she had felt like her heart had stopped beating.

When she reached the train station, she got in line to purchase her ticket to go home, glancing around at the people in line and the beauty of the Rockies surrounding her.

"Where to?" the old man behind the counter asked.

"Chicago," she said.

"The train to Chicago leaves on Sunday and Tuesday mornings."

"What? That's the soonest?"

"Yes, Ma'am."

"But I want to leave now," she demanded.

"Lady, I don't make the schedules," he said. "Do you want a ticket or not?"

That meant returning to Ethan and the ranch. That meant trying to find a ride back, as there was no way she could ride or walk by herself.

"No, but what time does it leave?"

"Nine o'clock. Don't be late," he said.

Walking away from the train platform, she now could purchase clothing that she was so badly needing, and she wanted to get him something as well. After all, he'd taken care of her these last few weeks. He'd been gentle, caring, and she could spend the rest of her money on the items she needed as well as Ethan. But she had to save enough to purchase her train ticket.

Hurrying across the street, she stepped inside the dress shop.

"May I help you?"

"Yes, I'm needing a new dress," she told the woman. "And also some pantaloons and a nightgown."

"Certainly. Are you new in town?"

"Yes, I'm Beth Fraser, Ethan Fraser's wife."

The woman's mouth dropped open, and her face went white. "Ethan married?"

Beth looked up from the garments she'd been inspecting on a table and gazed at the woman. She was young, pretty, and around Ethan's age. Could she be the girlfriend he'd given up?

"What's your name?" Beth asked.

"Alyssa," she answered softly.

Yes, this was the girl Ethan had been thinking of asking to dinner. Beth didn't want to hurt her. It wasn't Alyssa's fault Mama Fraser had gotten a bee in her bonnet and insisted her sons marry right away.

"We were married three weeks ago by his brother," Beth replied gently.

The woman's mouth dropped open for the briefest of time. Then she became all businesslike. "Let's get you started in a dressing room."

Beth carried a handful of clothes and walked with Alyssa to the back of the store. Why did it feel wrong that she'd had to be the one to tell Alyssa Ethan was no longer available? Especially since she was leaving town next week.

~

Beth and Ethan knocked on the parsonage, where Ruby and Gideon were living. After a disappointing afternoon, Beth was hardly in the mood to visit the couple, but she had no choice. First, she'd met the woman Ethan had been courting, and while she was probably a lovely young woman, Beth had felt jealous. Why should she feel jealous of the girl when she would soon be returning home?

Yet, the woman was nice, she was pretty, and Beth could see how she would have made Ethan a lovely bride. Much better suited to him than Beth was, and that rankled her big time. She was a Chicago debutante and this lady was a store clerk. Ethan had gotten a great bride, so why did she feel so worthless?

And before that, she'd had the frustrating visit to the train station. Sure, she now knew where and when to buy a ticket, but there was no guarantee she could convince Ethan to return to town next Sunday.

The only good thing was that she had indeed bought a new dress, new undergarments, and a nightgown, though the styles had been horribly out of season.

The front door opened, and Gideon smiled at them warmly, his brows raising at the sight of Beth. "Come in, come in. Let me have your coats. Ruby is in the kitchen. She'll be out soon."

They walked into the quaint little house, and Gideon took their coats. Beth glanced around and couldn't help but think surely, Gideon could do better than this. Why, this was barely more than a cottage. Sure, it was homey, had three bedrooms, but it was nothing compared to her home in Chicago.

Why had she believed that the people in town would be more like what she was use to in Chicago? She wasn't that picky but her life was so much different from the people in Angel Springs.

"Beth, why don't you go see if Ruby needs help?" Ethan said.

"I'm sure she's fine. I'll just get in the way." She glanced at him. The woman hadn't asked for help. Besides, this was why the preacher needed servants. They were supposed to fix dinner, not the women.

Beth didn't have a clue as to what she could do to help Ruby. She was barely functional in a kitchen. They were guests and guests did not wander into the kitchen. They were to be greeted in the parlor, served tea until the food was ready. Then the ladies would be escorted to the table by the gentlemen. She'd been raised that this was the proper structure for a dinner party.

Frustration filled her as she sat there fuming because the train wouldn't leave for another week. Another week of living on the ranch, milking cows, gathering eggs and learning to cook. Another week of being with Ethan. Of risking him sweeping her off her feet again. Of risking her heart.

Gideon raised his brows but remained silent. "I'll get us some tea. Perhaps Beth could pour."

"Certainly, I know how to do that." Though, at home a servant would have brought out the tea and given her the tray, but not here in the West. No, everything had to be done by hand. Or at least with the Fraser boys it did.

Ruby appeared at the door. "Dinner is ready. If you'll all come to the kitchen, we can eat. Well, as soon as Gideon carves the roast."

"Ethan and Beth, how are you two?" Ruby asked as she hugged each one.

Beth stared at the young woman's swollen belly. From the looks of it she'd hidden her pregnancy very well during the trip. No wonder the girl had seemed tired and without much personality. She'd been in hiding. Beth's own stomach tightened with fear, as she stared at her sister-in-law. She could very well be expecting at this moment too. This was what happened when you were intimate with your husband. You found yourself in the family way. Being pregnant would definitely change her plans.

Beth didn't know how to respond. She felt awkward. Ruby had appeared chunky, but her stomach had not been protruding like it was now. She couldn't help but wonder how understanding Gideon was of being saddled with another man's child.

"We can see how you are." Ethan eyed her stomach. "When will the little one arrive?"

"The end of December or there about."

"Oh, wouldn't it be wonderful to have a Christmas baby?" Beth said, doing her best to be excited. Pregnancy frightened her. Babies terrified her.

She couldn't get pregnant. She just couldn't. "You could name it Christian or Christina." Beth didn't know what else to say. They'd just gotten married, and suddenly, Gideon was the father of a child that obviously wasn't his, and Ruby had let him marry her without knowing she was expecting. At home, this would have been a huge scandal.

"We haven't talked about names yet. Come let's eat while the food is hot." Ruby pointed to the kitchen, leading them to the table.

Gideon had the roast with its nice red center on the table, several slices already cut.

"Everything looks wonderful, Ruby," Ethan said.

Beth watched her husband sit across from their hostess, Gideon to her right. Beth was astonished at the lack of formal dishes. Even for a luncheon, you used your best china. Surely even a preacher could afford more than what Gideon was offering Ruby. If he'd been Beth's husband, she would have insisted on redecorating the small house and purchasing all new dishes.

But she was quickly learning that even in town, formality was not followed in the West and being with her sister-in-law just reinforced the fear that was bubbling up inside her threatening to spill. She was supposed to be on that train headed to Chicago. Headed back to the life she was accustomed to. But here she sat staring at a woman's burgeoning belly afraid she could be pregnant. Afraid of being trapped.

And secretly that thought thrilled and terrified her at the same time. All of her plans would be for naught if she was carrying Ethan's child. All of her plans would be naught if she fell in love with him. She couldn't be tied here forever.

"Thank you. I do try. Mama Fraser taught me to make the gravy. Her little tricks make it come out perfect every time, and Gideon does like gravy. I think he'd eat it for breakfast, dinner, and supper if I made it."

Sliding her eyes to Ruby, Beth couldn't wait any longer to ask the question that was eating at her. "So when did your husband pass away?" She picked up her knife and fork and took a bite of the tender meat.

The men bristled at her comment and even Ruby seemed surprised. She was only trying to make conversation with Ruby and didn't intend to insult her. This was all such a shock. She'd never been around a pregnant woman before. She was an only child. She'd never seen an expecting woman and frankly, she was rather scared by the very idea of a baby growing inside her. But then a part of her wanted a child. Wanted to be a mother.

"Beth," said Gideon, "in this house, we pray before eating."

"Oh, I'm sorry." Sighing, she put her fork down and bowed her head. "Go ahead."

"Thank you, Father, for the food set before us and for all the blessings you give to us every day. Amen."

"Amen," repeated Ethan and Ruby.

Beth resisted rolling her eyes, though the urge was certainly there. "Can we eat now?"

"Yes," replied Gideon. "We may eat this fine meal Ruby has prepared."

Good grief, the man's wife was pregnant, and he made her do all the work. That was just unconscionable. Did any of the Fraser's believe in servants? Was every house in town like this, with the women doing all the work?

Gideon and Ethan kept up the conversation during the meal, while Ruby and Beth listened. Beth's question hung in the air between the two women, and Ruby never answered her. Why would she keep the date of his death a secret, unless there really wasn't a husband?

"Aren't you scared?" whispered Beth, knowing it wasn't delivering the baby that frightened her as much as the realization this would eventually happen to her, if she continued to have relations with Ethan. It had to stop. They couldn't be together again, or else she could get on that train to Chicago expecting his child. "I've heard delivery is very painful."

"A little," admitted Ruby, "but I wouldn't give up this little life in me for anything."

"It's nice Gideon is willing to take on such responsibility." The man was going to raise another man's child. Yes, he was a preacher, and hopefully, that made him a decent guy, but still he could help his wife and hire her some servants—a nurse…someone to be here when her time came.

"Yes," Ruby said, not looking at Beth.

When the meal was over, Ruby jumped up. "Who wants pie and who wants cobbler?"

"Both," Gideon and Ethan said together.

She cleared the dishes from the table as Beth relaxed in her chair, glancing around the small kitchen. She wanted to help Ruby, she really did, but she didn't know what to do. At the ranch Milly took care of the kitchen clean up. And was it polite to jump up and start carrying dishes off the table? In all her life, she'd never had to help clear the table. Never. She felt torn and helpless. Not one book she'd ever read on manners mentioned what to do when there were no servants present.

Ruby brought both desserts to the table with a knife and pie server and a large spoon for the cobbler. Then she gathered small plates and bowls, along with a jar full of sweet cream.

She really did like Ruby, but why did all the other women seem to try too hard to make their husbands happy? But then again, the other women all had wanted husbands and planned on staying forever. She was only here until she could catch a train home.

"Let's go sit in the parlor while the women folk clean up." Ethan and Gideon stood, and so did Beth. She followed the men into the parlor.

Ethan turned and stared at her. "Aren't you going to go help Ruby?"

What would she do, but get in the woman's way? But she wasn't about to tell Ethan in front of his brother. They all thought she was stuck up as it was. This would only confirm what everyone believed about her. She was a spoiled princess who didn't know anything.

She gazed at him. This was the reason why Ruby needed servants. Beth didn't know the first thing about how to clean the dishes, and she really didn't want to learn. They had ranch hands back at the Circle F that scrubbed dishes. Ruby and Gideon needed to hire someone.

"No," she said and followed the men into the parlor.

Gideon glared at her, and Beth wanted to tell him to quit being so cheap and get his wife some help.

Finally, after another thirty minutes, Ethan stood. "I guess we better get back to the ranch before dark falls."

Gideon stood, and the two men shook hands. Ruby came in from the kitchen, carrying a hand towel. Beth shook her head. She'd never realized until this moment, just how spoiled she really was. Even at the ranch she'd not had to clean the dishes and whatever chore they gave her, she'd had help. But to walk into another woman's home and be expected to help with the serving. Why she'd never dreamed of doing such a thing.

A shiver raced down her spine, and she couldn't wait until she returned to Chicago and back to a life filled with servants. A sense of ache filled her. A life without Ethan.

"Thanks, Ruby, for the lovely meal," Ethan said, leaning over and kissing her on the cheek.

"You're so welcome. Come back any time," she replied.

"It was delightful," Beth lied wishing she'd never come to town with Ethan today. This only showed how out place she really was. She knew nothing about being a hostess in the West or even being a good guest.

"Good bye, Gideon," Beth said, and her brother-in-law nodded his head toward her. Well, that was certainly rude.

Chapter Eleven

Outside, Ethan helped Beth up into the wagon. "What's wrong with you?" he said in a huff. "Can't you see she's pregnant? Why didn't you offer to help her in the kitchen?"

She turned and glared at him. "Is it my problem her husband is too cheap to hire her servants?"

He called to the horses, and they started down the street away from the parsonage. From the set of his jaw and his flashing brown eyes, she could tell she'd made him angry by refusing to help. It was just another example of how different their lives were. In his, everyone worked, and in hers the servants took care of the family. Missing the train today had brought it all back. Everything she'd given up to become a mail-order bride.

"Beth, do you think we're going to have servants once we have our house built?"

"Of course. I'm not going to do all the housework."

He pulled the wagon to a stop and turned to stare at her. "I know you come from a privileged childhood. But did you think you were going to come to Colorado, marry me and have the same type of life?"

She swallowed, her eyes filling with tears as her stomach clenched. She hadn't given any thought to her decision to leave Chicago and her pampered life behind. She'd only run as fast as she could out of town, to escape a wedding she couldn't get out of from a man who didn't really want her. Being a mail-order bride had seemed like the perfect solution, and now she found herself on a ranch, where you had to work for a living. She didn't know how to take care of herself or anyone else for that matter. Sure she was learning, but no one had taught her how to be a good guest. At home her behavior would have been acceptable, even expected, but here she was once again the outcast.

"I just ran, Ethan. I didn't think about the consequences or what would be expected of me."

"Let me tell you the reality of life here," he said, taking a deep breath. "People have to work for a living. Women help one another. You're expected to assist, especially a pregnant woman, in the kitchen with the cooking and the cleanup afterward."

Her mother had held many a tea and dinner, but she'd never expected her guests to help with cleanup after they'd shared a meal, did no one understand she didn't know the new rules? She was still trying to live like she had in Chicago. But things had changed. This was her first outing away from the ranch. At least there she knew the rules, here she lapsed back into what she was familiar with. Which only showed how different they were.

"Don't you think that's a little unfair? You men sit there and get to talk while the women are busy washing dishes and putting up the food after the meal? We cook and have to clean as well." If they were going to fight about what really should be left to their servants, then she was going to show him it just wasn't fair the way it was now.

"Do you think it's fair the men have to go out and work the ranch every day, so you have food to put on the table for us and a roof over your head?"

She huffed and stared at the man she'd married. Certainly her father had never held a job that was as dangerous or grueling as Ethan's. He'd dealt with other men who owned large companies, and they'd worked out all kinds of financial deals. Sure, he'd been busy, but his work was nothing like Ethan's.

"I've never had to worry about a roof over my head. I've never had to worry about food being on the table as the servants always took care of us. I'm learning." Their time together had been grueling as they taught her the basics of ranch life. The training had not all been unpleasant, but when did it stop? What more did he want from her?

"Well, you need to learn to think about someone other than yourself."

"And just what do you mean by that?"

"You expect everyone to take care of you, but it's not just about you. It's supposed to be a partnership. We all take care of each other. We help out. If you don't know how to do something, ask. We'll show you how."

She swallowed, feeling tears on the tips of her lashes. He made her sound awful, and she really did expect people to take care of her. It was what she was used to, what she'd known all her life. But servants took care of her out of necessity, Ethan's care taking had been different. It had been personal. Not since her mother had she felt genuinely cherished.

The experience had been powerful enough to frighten her.

"I'm sorry. I'm trying to understand and fit in, and sometimes, I don't think and I go back on my instincts. I was shocked at seeing Ruby so far pregnant."

"And that's when you should have realized she would need your help in the kitchen."

"Like I would know how to help her? I've never washed dishes. And we all know how great my cooking is."

He clicked to the horses, and the wagon began to move again. "Just be more thoughtful of the people around you. In time, your cooking will come along. Now, let's get home. We've had quite a day."

With a sigh, Beth grabbed onto the wagon as it lurched forward. Once again, she'd displeased her husband, and he'd found her less than favorable. She couldn't wait to leave and catch that train to return to the world she was accustomed to.

She'd never realized how her life was unusual or how spoiled and habituated she was to the riches her wealth provided. But now, now she'd had a harsh dose of reality, and while there were things about this life she enjoyed, she couldn't wait to get back to her previous life.

~

A week passed and Ethan watched his wife trying to fit into the routine. He knew she was making an effort, but still, it was frustrating to see how little she really knew about life. Sure he'd heard of women like her, but he'd never thought he would be married to someone so helpless.

Walking into the office, he watched his mother behind the desk. Her head was bent over the accounting books, and he could tell she was figuring numbers. A few days ago, she'd injured her ankle and stayed mainly in the house, trying to let the limb heal.

He sank into the chair across from her. She glanced up. Their relationship still hadn't returned to what it had been before she'd taken it upon herself to find him a bride—a bride who she'd not carefully checked out. Someone who had no idea of how to live on a ranch.

"Hello, son," she said with a sigh. "I called you in today because I wanted to first apologize. You were right. I should never have chosen a wife for you. That was your decision, and I hope you will eventually forgive me for putting you in such an awkward situation with a woman who is not prepared to take care of you and any children you may have. I'm sorry."

What had brought about this sudden realization? Yes, he'd been furious the decision to marry had been taken from him. Yes, his wife was less than ideal when it came to knowing how to run a household. But she was learning, she was trying and since she came from a background where she didn't have to cook, or clean, he felt like she'd come a long way.

And there was something about her sweet spirit that he was beginning to really care about Beth. There was an innocence about her that made her actions sometimes laughable and sometimes just frustrating as hell. But still she was his wife. And he felt honor bound to protect her, even from his mother.

Did his mother think that by apologizing he would forgive her?

"What's done is done, Mother."

Sure, he hadn't wanted Beth, but every day they grew closer and well, she made him laugh. Though, he wished she would learn how to help others better than she had been. Until she came into his life, he'd never realized how much women helped each other, and Beth needed to learn more about helping her sisters-in-law.

"I did some research, and if the marriage hasn't been consummated, you would still be able to get it annulled."

He threw back his head laughing. "First, you wanted me to marry the woman, and now, you're telling me I should get the marriage annulled?"

Frowning, she leaned backward in her chair and stared at him. "I'm giving you a way out of a bad situation. It's your choice. You're the only one of my children who hasn't been able to see I was doing what I thought was best for you. And your wife is the weakest of the women. I don't know if she will ever fit in."

A warning trickle of anger zipped along his spine. As Beth's husband, it was his duty to defend her, and he wouldn't let anyone insult his wife. Not even his mother. Now that he was married, he wasn't about to give up his wife.

"I may not have wanted this marriage, and in fact, I still resent the way you didn't take my wants into consideration but just herded all of us into a wedding, but I'm standing by Beth."

"Son, she doesn't belong here. I doubt she'll stay. She's already tried to leave right after a blizzard. Your brother, Jamie, and I believe she will bolt just as soon as you take her to town."

His stomach clenched at the thought of her leaving, and red-hot anger fueled his blood. He'd taken Beth to town and she hadn't run. Why was it his mother hit on the very fear that sometimes woke him in the middle of the night? What if Beth ran again? What if she died out in the snow trying to escape from him?

"She may not belong just yet, but she's learning our ways. She wants to be a part of our clan but doesn't know how. Is this why Jamie's telling me to wait a year before the ranch can afford to build us a home?"

His mother stared at him. "I don't think she'll ever fit in. You would be smart to cut your losses and see about annulling the marriage." She hadn't answered him, which told him he was right about the new house.

"No. You don't have the right to tell me I should end this union. You still haven't learned your lesson, Mother. What Beth and I decide is none of your business, and you would do well to support my wife. The marriage can't be annulled."

His mother sighed. "What can I do to resolve this situation between us? What's it going to take?"

"The most important thing is for you to never assume that just because you're my mother you can make my decisions. I'm a grown man. I take care of Beth and myself, and she and I work together. If you want us to stay, then help me convince Jamie there is sufficient money to build us a house. Beth is staying. You picked her, and I would suggest you do everything you can to help her belong here, including getting us a home."

Frowning, his mother looked at the ledger in front of her then raised her eyes to his. "I'm sorry this hasn't turned out like I thought it would, and it's created a rift between us. I'll do what I can to convince your brother you need a house." She licked her lips nervously. "There is a Grange meeting tomorrow night. Your brother is being sworn in as president. You should be there to support him."

Ethan shook his head. Since he'd married and requested they build a home for his new wife, Jamie and he had not gotten along. Now, not only was his mother trying to heal the rift between them, but she wanted him to get past his anger with his brother. But like his mother, Jamie thought Beth would not be staying, that she would eventually return to Chicago and the society she belonged to—Ethan's biggest fear.

"I'll support my brother when he agrees to build my home and accept my wife."

"Ethan, Jamie just doesn't want to spend resources on a building you may never need."

Anger gripped him, and before he unleashed the fury on his mother, he quickly stood. "You're both wrong. Beth will still be here, and you're going to feel ashamed when your grandchildren are being raised in a barn."

Turning on his heel, he strode out the door and hurried home to Beth. His family had to be wrong. They just had to be because he was starting to really care for his wife.

~

Ethan walked across the yard to the barn, his boots sinking into the mud, taking deep breaths to release the anger he felt toward his mother. The woman still hadn't learned the lesson of not interfering, and he wondered if she ever would. His boots were covered with slush and mud and even some snow, as he stomped his way to the barn.

In December, the mud would be frozen solid until spring, when once again the big thaw would occur. By that time, he hoped his wife would be expecting their first child, she'd be madly in love with him, and she wouldn't think about leaving to return to Chicago.

It was a worry, a constant nagging thought, that his world was nothing like hers, and she would soon tire of all the work and flee back to the place where her life was easy.

In the barn, he hurried up the stairs, eager to see if she was in the loft. Supper would soon be served, and he liked escorting her over to the main house, where they took their meals most of the time.

Entering the loft, the aroma of something baking wafted from the oven. Beth was changing clothes, and he could see her shadow behind the screen. She was humming a tune he didn't recognize, but she had set their little table with dishes, and everything appeared ready for supper. His wife had successfully made her first meal without almost burning down the barn.

Tiptoeing, he crossed the room and snuck up behind her. Wrapping his arms around her, he nuzzled her neck, his pulse racing at the feel of her in his arms, her scent surrounding him. Maybe tonight she would let him make love to her once again.

She jerked in his arms. "Ethan, what are you doing?"

"I'm kissing my half-dressed wife after a long day of checking on the herd. What are you doing?"

Leaning against him, she relaxed and gave him access to her throat. "Well, I cooked a pot roast, some potatoes and have dinner all ready for us."

"Does this mean we're eating alone?" he asked.

She turned to face him. "Is that okay? I was tired of sitting around the table with the family."

He squeezed her tight, enjoying her feminine curves against his body. "I think it sounds great. In fact, I think I'll clean up and get ready to eat. It smells wonderful."

"Thanks, I hope it turns out okay. Milly helped me get it ready."

He released her then walked to the bowl and pitcher to wash his hands. In a few moments, he glanced up as Beth took their dinner out of the oven. It looked delicious. Even if their dinner was tough as cow hide, he would tell her how wonderful it tasted because he didn't want to discourage her. She was trying so hard to please him, and she deserved some appreciation.

The glow of the lantern was bright in the room. Sitting at the table, he let her serve him. She spooned up some roast beef, potatoes, and gravy. The smell was enough to make his stomach growl.

She sat across from him and watched nervously, her eyes radiating concern as he took the first bite.

The meat was succulent and practically fell apart, it was so tender. "Very good, honey. You keep cooking like this, and we'll soon be preparing food for the entire ranch." Relief flooded his midsection. He was thankful he didn't have to lie. The food truly tasted great.

"I don't think so," Beth said, taking a bite. "This *is* good."

"You did very well. I knew you could cook."

"Thank you," she said. "When I arrived, there were a lot of things I didn't know I could ever do, and now I look around, and I'm doing pretty well."

Ethan swelled with pride. She was doing better, and if she sounded this pleased, then she wouldn't be leaving. Finally, maybe, she was beginning to fit in around here. Now, he had to get his family to accept her and not stand in her way. "I'm very proud of you. You've learned a lot."

She smiled, obviously pleased and that made him feel good. Maybe they were getting over this newlywed hurtle and could experience the love his mother and father had shared. He did care about Beth. In fact, he knew if he let himself he could love her, but was afraid. Afraid of her fulfilling his brother's prediction and running away, leaving him behind.

She had run from her first wedding. Would she run from her current husband too?

"What did your mother have to say?" she asked. "I heard her tell Spunky she wanted to speak with you. How's her ankle today?"

"Her ankle is better but still swollen. She wanted us to go to my brother's swearing in ceremony for the Grange." He wasn't about to tell her the real reason his mother had wanted to speak to him. Beth had no business knowing everyone in the family expected her to bolt as soon as she could get back to town. Of course she'd had an opportunity last time and hadn't jumped on the train.

"Oh, we should go support him."

"No, I don't think so."

"Are you and he still not speaking?"

Shrugging his shoulders, Ethan didn't really feel like talking to Beth about Jamie. If she knew the real reason for them not getting a house, then she would have another excuse to run.

"You deserve better than living in a barn. You could be expecting, and I will not raise my children here in this loft. It's not fair," he said, knowing the real reason they'd not been approved for building a house. A place she could make into a home.

"It's not that bad. Sure, it's small, and with children, it would be difficult, but it's funny a month ago I was living in a mansion, and now, I'm quite content living in a loft in a barn. Suzy Smithers would certainly have some tattling to do if she learned of my change in status."

Ethan cringed. There was no way he could ever give her the life she had with her father. It just wasn't possible.

He reached across the table and picked up her hand. "I'm glad you're here with me. Not in Chicago. And I'm proud to call you my wife. I'll do everything I can to give you back a portion of what you lost in Chicago." He lifted her hand to his mouth and kissed it tenderly.

"I don't want what I left behind in Chicago," she said softly, her eyes misting with tears.

Grinning at her, his heart filled to bursting, with joy. Maybe his family was wrong, and Beth was serious about staying here, toughening up, and learning to live the life of a rancher's wife. He hoped so because every day he grew to like his wife more and more. So much in fact, it scared him. He could no longer imagine a life without her by his side.

There's a dance next weekend at the Grange Hall. If the weather holds off, do you want to go?"

She smiled at him. "Can we stay in town?"

"Yes, they're holding it Saturday night. I thought we'd spend the night and then come home after church on Sunday."

"I'd love to go dancing with you, husband."

Somehow the way she said the word husband spread warmth through him better than a roaring fire. "Usually the family goes."

"As long as we have our own hotel room."

"Oh, we will," he said softly, knowing exactly what he wanted to do in that hotel room with her.

"Great. That will be fun."

"If I help you clean up, will you play checkers with me?" For some reason, he wanted to play a game, and he wanted to do it with his wife by his side. Maybe a little friendly competition where she lost and wound up in his bed again. He missed her sleeping by his side, curling around her and waking up next to her.

"I'd love to beat you at checkers," she said, wiping away the tears from the corners of her eyes.

"That, Mrs. Fraser, sounds like a challenge."

"Oh, it's not a challenge. It's a promise that you will not go away unscathed by my checker playing skills."

"What does the winner get?" he asked.

She smiled. "The entire bed to herself tonight."

Since they'd gone to town, she'd returned to sleeping on the sofa, and he wanted her back in his bed with him.

"No," he said. "I think the winner gets sex."

A frown crossed her face. "No."

"Why not?"

"It just seems wrong to be betting our bodies."

"But it would be so much fun, and we're married."

Her brows drew together as she stared at him, tilting her head to the side. "Okay, if you win, you get sex. But if I win, I get a nice luxurious bath with hot water brought to me by my husband."

"With me in the tub with you." That would be fun.

"No, you'll be bringing me hot water, and you'll attend your brother's swearing in ceremony," she said, then walked away.

For a moment, Ethan sat stunned as he watched his wife stroll off, clearly ending the negotiations. Now he had to win, as he didn't want to attend Jamie's swearing in ceremony. Plus, the idea of wrapping his body around hers was plenty enough incentive to win.

Chapter Twelve

Beth glanced at her husband over the checkers. What the poor man didn't know was she'd been her school's champion checkers player at the very young age of ten. The girls had given her a hard time, but she'd loved being the top one in her class, and she'd shown up all of the boys. Maybe that was why none of them had ever pursued her. Of course, shortly after her tenth birthday, her father had packed her up and shipped her off to The Refined Arts School for Young Ladies, where she'd learned how to host tea parties and social functions and only received a basic education in academic subjects.

Ethan stared at his checkers, searching for his best move, but what he didn't realize was she'd led him to where he had only one move, before her king captured many of his pieces.

"Did you play checkers much?" he asked nonchalantly.

Inside, she was laughing, but on the outside, she played coy. "Oh, occasionally my father and I used to play."

"What about your fiancé? Did you play checkers with him?"

"He was my father's friend. I know they often played together, but I was not included." She glanced over at her husband and remembered how his hands harassed her breasts, his lips seared her skin. Heat flowed through her body, centering in her middle. She could not act on these urges he invoked.

Ethan was a handsome young, virile man who had been more kind to her than her father's friend, her first fiancé, yet she planned on purchasing a train ticket just as soon as she and Ethan got back to town.

Leaving Ethan would be hard. She liked her husband.

In one swift move, she took his last three checkers. His mouth dropped open, as he stared at her with surprise.

"Do you want to make it two out of three?" she questioned.

"Why do I think I've just been had? I'm a pretty good player, but I've never been beat like that before."

A smile curved her lips. While he set up the board again, she asked, "Have you ever considered leaving the ranch?"

"Sure. I even went east for a while, but I missed the Colorado mountains, and I got tired of so many people."

He would hate Chicago. She knew it, but still, if she could take him with her, she would. But how did you convince a man to follow you home without giving away your secret desire to escape?

"Why do you ask?"

"I just wondered if you would take me back to Chicago to visit my father."

"Of course. And you're welcome to invite him here any time," he said, his brows drawn, his jaw tight. "But I was under the impression you left on not so good terms."

"I did, but I hope eventually he'll understand I could not marry Henry. I didn't love him and—" The memory of what she'd seen that night sent a shiver up her spine. She'd never imagined.

"What sent you running, Beth?" he asked softly. "I know you're not the type of woman who easily gives up on something. So whatever it was had to be huge."

She moved her checker, placing his king in jeopardy. This was her game, her one thing she could do very well. She and Ethan were having a lovely time together, and she just wanted to gaze at him and dream. For soon, she would be gone, and that thought left her sad.

"I don't want to talk about Henry. I'd rather beat you at checkers, so I can have my bath, and you, dear husband, can attend your brother's swearing in ceremony." She gave him her best stern look.

"Do you promise to tell me someday?"

She laughed, trying to keep the bitterness out of her voice. No, she hadn't loved him, but she'd never considered Henry to be what she'd seen that night. His dishonesty had stung the most. It was definitely a tale of pure diabolical craziness, one she'd never thought either man capable of.

"Yes, one of these days, I'll tell you why I ran from that wedding, besides the fact my fiancé was old enough to be my father. But not tonight, when you are about to fix me a most luxurious bath."

There was no reason why Ethan needed to know about Henry, and she wasn't certain he would believe her. Her father hadn't; he'd accused her of lying and had questioned her motive for being deceitful about his best friend. But she could never erase the image from her brain, and it had been enough to make her realize she would never marry that man. So she'd left that night and agreed to be a mail-order bride, thinking it would be easy. She'd taken the place of a girl who'd decided at the last moment she couldn't leave Chicago. Beth knew she'd gotten lucky that night.

But this was the hardest thing she'd ever done, and now, all she could think about was how she would be hurting Ethan. And he was a victim in this terrible game.

"You're not going to let me win, are you?" he asked.

She almost snorted with laughter, as she gazed at her husband. Why hadn't he been the man she was supposed to marry in Chicago, instead of a creepy old man who didn't like women? "No."

After capturing his last checkers, she looked up at him. She really wanted him to mend this rift with his brother. She knew it was because of her that he was insisting on building this house, yet she wouldn't be here to enjoy it.

His brother was much more important. That was why she'd brought Jamie into the checker game.

"Tomorrow night, I guess you're going to be supporting your oldest brother at his swearing in ceremony. Make my bath extra warm, please."

~

A few days later, Beth walked through the fresh snow, trying to lift her skirt high enough to keep it from becoming a muddy mess. The wind blew sending swirls of snow across the frozen ice that crunched beneath her feet. Another snowstorm had hit the ranch, and this time they'd almost lost two members of the Fraser family.

When Olivia instructed Jake to finish his studies, he'd run off to keep from doing the schoolwork and almost died. Like the caring mother she was, Olivia had gone after the boy, even with a looming storm. During the height of the blizzard, they'd all feared the two were dead, but Olivia had found the little boy and kept both of them safe until the men had rescued them. The ranch had been in complete turmoil, with everyone's nerves on edge as they waited for the pair to be located.

Thank God Jamie had found his wife and son and brought them back to the ranch two days ago. Now, Beth walked the distance to their home to check on Olivia to see if there was anything she could do to help her sister-in-law. Beth had been worried sick with Olivia and Jake missing, and she realized how close she'd gotten to the people who lived here.

As she entered the house, envy roared its ugly head. Jamie's family had a home and didn't live in a barn. Then she reminded herself she wouldn't be here long enough to see a house built.

"Good morning." Beth strolled through the back door.

Cat ran to her. The little girl was still rowdy, but since the incident in the pigpen, she seemed to mind Olivia better and had even grown attached to the woman.

"Where's your mom?" Beth asked.

"She's in bed. She's not feeling good."

Beth hurried to the bedroom, where she found Olivia huddled beneath the covers. "Are you all right?"

The woman's teeth were chattering. "I can't get warm…and my head is killing me."

"Where do you keep the quilts?"

"In the trunk sitting against the wall."

She pulled out a blanket and piled it on Olivia. The woman's complexion was a ghastly white. She'd spent days out in the elements protecting Jake, and Beth feared the ordeal had taxed Olivia's health. "What if I fix you some hot tea?"

"That sounds good."

Cat stared at the woman who had taken the place of her dead mother. Her eyes filled with concern.

"Why don't you help me, Cat?"

"Okay." The little girl walked into the kitchen with Beth and tugged on her skirt.

"What, honey?"

"She's not going to die, is she? I don't want to lose another momma."

Beth's heart wrenched at the way this small child had already experienced death once and was afraid it could happen again. "Of course not. She's just ill. You've gotten sick before."

"Yes, but my real momma died."

Beth pulled the child to her and held her small body against her own, offering comfort. She'd really grown to love this little girl. "My real mom died as well, but just because someone gets sick doesn't mean they're going to die. She just doesn't feel well. Let's take her some hot tea and see if we can't make her feel better."

"Okay," the little girl said, her voice hesitant.

After releasing her, Beth walked to the stove and put the kettle on. "Get the tea out. I've put the water on to boil."

Cat found the tea and brought it to Beth.

"Where's your brother?"

"He's in his room, doing his numbers. Daddy told him he better obey Olivia from now on. Since he got home, he's been studying very hard."

"Good. What about you? Have you done your schoolwork yet?"

Cat frowned then shrugged her shoulders, clearly an indication she'd not done her studies. She wasn't old enough to really focus on learning, but while Olivia had her brother, sitting down and working Cat had wanted to attend school, so she was learning to draw her letters. It kept the child occupied and out of trouble.

"You know I was thinking maybe we could work on a dress for your new doll after you get your schoolwork done. I have some leftover material we could use."

Her eyes widened. "I'll do my schoolwork just as soon as we take Momma her tea."

Beth smiled. She would never have children, and after she left, she would miss Cat something fierce, just like she'd miss Ethan. She pushed the thoughts out of her mind, as the kettle whistled. Using a hot pad, she lifted it off the fire.

Once the tea had steeped for a couple of minutes, she found the honey and dropped a teaspoon into the hot liquid, hoping it would soothe Olivia.

"Can I take it in to Momma?"

"Sorry, honey, but it's too hot for you to carry. Grab me a washcloth, and you can take her a soothing wet cloth."

"Okay." Cat ran to the closet and came back with a rag.

Beth poured some cool water over the cloth, wrung it out, and gave it to the child.

"Give this to Olivia when we get to the bedroom."

Cat nodded and followed Beth to see her ailing mother.

Even in the short time they were gone, Olivia seemed to have grown weaker, and her breathing sounded congested like she was struggling for every bit of air she could get into her lungs. She lay against the pillows, her skin pale, and her eyes shut.

Slowly, she opened her lids when Beth and Cat came into the room.

Jamie's wife was getting worse, much worse, and that frightened Beth. "We brought you some tea," she offered with forced cheer.

"And a cool rag," Cat said, eager to help take care of her new momma. "Are you okay?"

Olivia reached out and took the rag from her stepdaughter. "I'll be okay. Right now, I just don't feel well."

Beth set the tea on the bedside table. "Cat, why don't you get started on your schoolwork, so we can make that dress for your doll?"

"Okay," she said, giving her stepmother another glance before she skipped out the door.

After she left, Beth pulled a chair close to the bed. "I thought I would stay and watch over them today and let you rest. You've been through a lot, and your body is demanding sleep. Maybe you'll feel better." Actually, she was very frightened for Olivia.

"Thanks, Beth. My strength just seems to have drained from me. What did you promise Cat to get such a reaction?"

Beth shrugged. "I told her we would make her dolly a dress if she did her homework."

Olivia smiled. "You're good with children. I think you need a few of your own."

"Oh no, not now," Beth said, thinking of how she would soon be leaving the ranch.

A coughing spell hit Olivia, and Beth rushed to find her a handkerchief. When she finished, she noticed the rag was pink.

"When did you start coughing?" Beth asked, staring at the blood-tinged handkerchief, her heart beating fast as concern for her sister-in-law filled her. Cat and Jake needed a mother. They'd become much better children since Olivia had come into their lives. Jamie needed his wife, and Beth couldn't bear the ranch without Olivia.

"A couple of days ago."

"You're coughing up blood."

"That just started today. I'll be okay."

Olivia finished her tea, and Beth knew she needed to let her rest. "You sleep for a while."

"Thanks, Beth. I'll take a nap then get up to fix Jamie's supper."

Beth didn't think the woman would be getting up for several days, but she wasn't going to argue with Olivia. Instead, Beth would watch the children. "Holler if you need anything. I'll keep checking on you."

"Thanks." Olivia pulled the covers up to her neck and closed her eyes.

As Beth shut the door, she glanced back and noticed Olivia was already asleep, and her breathing sounded horrible, like with every breath she struggled to get enough air.

An hour later, Olivia was still sleeping, but Jamie had come back to the house for lunch. When he walked in and found Beth feeding his kids, his brows rose in alarm. "Where's Olivia?"

"When I came over this morning to check on her, she wasn't feeling well. I've been watching the children while she rested." Touching him on the arm, she led him down the hall toward the room where his wife lay ill, where Jake and Cat couldn't hear what she had to say.

"I think you need to send for the doctor," she said with concern. "She's coughing up blood. This hit her quick and hard."

He shook his head bewildered. "She said she didn't feel well this morning, but she acted like it was nothing."

"With her being exposed to the weather for several days, I worry she could have pneumonia, especially after I watched her cough." Beth slowly opened the door and peered inside, Olivia lay exactly like she'd left her several hours ago.

Her skin was china doll pale and looked almost ghostly white around her lips.

Jamie walked into the room and laid his hand on her forehead. "She's burning up."

Turning on her heel, Beth hurried back to the kitchen, where she poured a basin of cool water then returned to the bedroom. The rag Cat had placed on her mother's head was now warm. Beth soaked it in the water, wrung it out, and laid it across Olivia's forehead. She didn't open her eyes.

Running his hands through his hair, Jamie stared at his wife. "She wasn't near this sick this morning."

"I think it's time to send for the doctor."

Fear for her sister-in-law, her fellow mail-order bride had her wringing her hands. She didn't want anything to happen to poor Olivia.

"I think you're right."

Suddenly, Olivia started to cough, and her eyes opened part way as she grabbed the rag lying near her. When she finished, it was smattered with blood. Jamie glanced at

Beth, his eyes wide with fright. "I'll send someone to town right now."

~

Later that afternoon, Ethan waited with Beth inside Jamie and Olivia's parlor. Cat and Jake had been sent to stay with their grandmother until further notice. The doctor was in with Jamie and Olivia.

Ethan worried that once again his brother would have to bury a wife. Though he and Jamie had not reconciled their differences, he still cared about his brother and didn't want to see him suffer the loss of Olivia. He didn't know if Jamie loved his wife, but even Ethan had grown fond of the woman. She'd tamed Jamie's wild kids and seemed to have brought some order to his home. There was so much more she could accomplish here, and the thought of her dying just wasn't right.

Beth paced the floor. Ethan was proud of what she'd done. She'd come to the house and taken over the children and even told Jamie he should send for the doctor. She'd handled herself well.

Since their fight after leaving Ruby and Gideon's, she'd actually done much better. She seemed to be trying to fit into life at the ranch, and every day he was pleased at how she was changing right before their eyes. If he were wearing his brother's shoes right now, he'd be so upset by the possibility of Beth dying.

The bedroom door opened, and the doctor walked out with Jamie. Ethan watched as his older brother showed the doctor to the front door.

"Thanks for coming to see us, Dr. Miller. We'll see you tomorrow, unless I need you before then."

"Goodnight, Jamie," he said and tipped his hat to the rest of them before leaving.

"Pneumonia," Jamie said, turning to look at Beth. "Thank God he thinks we caught it early enough. But if I'd waited even twenty-four hours, he said he doesn't think she could have recovered."

Reaching out to Beth, Jamie pulled her into his arms. "Thank you. Twice now you've been a real sister to my family. You saved my daughter and now my wife. I can't thank you enough."

Ethan watched as Jamie hugged his wife, his chest filling with pride. No one had given his wife any credit when she came to the ranch, not even himself. But she was proving to them she was much stronger than they expected. She was turning into a woman he was so honored to call his wife. His heart was becoming involved, and somehow he'd made a great match, even when he hadn't wanted one.

Beth stepped back. "Thank you. I'm just so relieved she's going to be okay. Your children were very worried about her. Poor Cat was afraid Olivia was going to die. I think it would be a good idea for you to go tell them the doctor says she's going to be okay. I know they're frightened. Ethan and I won't leave until you get back, in case Olivia needs anything."

Jamie ran his hand through his hair. After taking a deep breath, he sighed and squirmed.

Ethan frowned. His big brother never fidgeted, unless he had something he didn't feel comfortable saying.

"Beth, Ethan. I owe you an apology."

Without a doubt, Ethan knew. Beth was finally going to get the acceptance she needed.

She asked, "Whatever for?"

"When you first came to the ranch, I didn't believe you would stay," Jamie confessed. "I thought you would get tired of being out here without the fancy lifestyle you were accustomed to. That's why I didn't want to commit to building a home for you. I didn't think you would last."

Anger rushed through Ethan, and his hands clenched into fists. This was why Jamie had never been friendly to Beth, even after she'd rescued Cat from the pigpen. He wondered if his other brothers felt the same way and thought Beth would soon tire and leave the ranch and Ethan.

Hell, he'd even questioned if she would stay himself. Now, he couldn't imagine her not here at his side. Taking a calming breath, he realized they were putting this behind them. Finally, his family was coming around to accepting the woman he'd married.

"I'm sorry, Ethan. Beth is a fine woman, and I'm proud to call you my sister. After the spring thaw, we'll build that home you two are wanting and get you out of the barn."

Beth hugged him. "Thanks, Jamie."

That was all she said, and Ethan was a little surprised she wasn't more excited. After complaining about the loft, he felt certain she would be jumping up and down with joy. They were going to soon have their own place without the smell of animals permeating the air.

Maybe because of how serious Olivia's condition was she was holding back, but he wasn't certain, and her calmness made him nervous.

Chapter Thirteen

Ethan was tired. He wanted to reach the loft, spend some time with his wife then crawl into bed. He and his brothers had spent the day hauling hay out to the cattle that were not close to the house, and for some reason, he felt every pound of hay he'd lifted in his muscles tonight.

As he crossed the yard to the barn, he saw his mother limping toward him. He didn't need another confrontation with her. He was tired of them arguing. What was done was done, yet he knew she still needed to know not to ever do anything like this again.

"Ethan!" she called, hobbling along.

He started walking toward her. "I don't think you should be out yet."

"Maybe not, but I needed to talk to you, and I was tired of sitting in that office with my foot propped up."

"Let me help you back to the house."

She gazed up at him, her eyes going wide.

"I know I've been upset with you, but you're still my mother, and I don't like to see you hurt."

"Thank you," she said softly, leaning against him as he turned her toward the house.

"So, what was so all-fire urgent you had to come to me?"

She stopped and put her hands on her hips. "It's time we healed this rift between us. Jamie and I discussed it, you and Beth are going to have a home built in the spring."

He nodded. "Thank you. But what else?"

"I'm sorry for taking matters into my own hands and finding you a wife. As much as I hate to say this, you're a man, and I should never have interfered."

"Thank you. What else?"

Sighing, she shook her head. "You are the most stubborn son a mother could ever have."

He smiled. "Continue."

"I'm sorry for trying to convince you to have your marriage annulled, but I did it because I wanted to see if you were falling in love with your wife. And I think you are. That showed me how invested you were in this union. And I'm pleased. I can see the changes in Beth, and I just hope and pray she will continue to grow into the wife my son deserves."

Wrapping his arm around his mother, he helped her toward the house, as he let her words fill his brain and his heart. Yes, he was falling in love with Beth, and while it frightened him because he didn't feel the same commitment from her, he also knew there was no stopping or holding back. Hopefully, she would soon catch up with him, and their marriage would become strong.

"You know I only wanted the same type of union you and Papa had. He may have died before we were ready to see him go, but I remember the love you two shared. I wanted to make certain I found a woman who could give me the same devotion you showed Papa."

His mother looped her arm around his waist. "That's what I want for all my sons. We can't expect results overnight, but I see the way you look at Beth. She's not immune, so I'm hoping in time you'll receive the love and devotion you deserve."

As they reached the steps leading into the house, he helped his mother up. Then they stopped and stared out at the land they both loved. "Your father and I wanted to leave a legacy. We wanted you boys and your children to make this ranch into an empire. I guess I got tired of waiting and worried I wouldn't live to see it happen, so I took things into my own hands, not thinking about how I was taking the choice of *who* away from you."

"Yes, you did. But I have to say, Mother, that even though Beth is not who I would have chosen, I think she's going to become a great partner. Things have a way of working out the way they should."

She smiled up at him. "So are you back to being my loving son?"

He laughed. "As long as you stay out of my business."

"I'll do my best, but now I'm going to be pressing you for grandchildren. I can't wait to see the babies you two create. And I can't wait see what you and your brothers do to the ranch."

He hugged her. "Let's start with the house then the grandbabies."

"I can hardly wait."

"Me too."

~

Olivia was feeling better, but she still hadn't regained her strength. She and Jamie opted out of attending the dance. Beth was disappointed, but she knew it was best for Olivia to continue growing stronger. Before leaving for town, she'd gone to their home early that morning to tell Olivia goodbye. While saying goodbye, Beth had felt tears gathering in her eyes at the thought of never seeing her sister-in-law again. Of all the women on the ranch, Olivia had been the kindest to Beth, and this morning when Beth had told her goodbye, Olivia hadn't realized it was for good.

Now, staring at the couples swirling on the floor, she understood even more about the social world of Angel Springs, Colorado. The women wore their finest calico, but their dresses were nothing compared to what the elite wore in Chicago. And the music was downright hokey compared to the grand orchestras or quartets that supplied the dance music at a social gathering.

Even though the quality was not the same, the people were enjoying themselves, and the crowd was lively and fun, and the women friendly. As Beth glanced around, she realized though she'd grown up with the best, this event was probably even more fun due to the relaxed atmosphere and the gaiety. People were actually having fun. Not simply pretending.

Mama Fraser motioned Beth over to the chair where she was sitting, her ankle still not completely healed. She took Beth's hand and held it for a moment. "Beth, I have to say something to you. Of the girls who married my sons, you were the one I doubted ever being happy at the ranch. You were more refined and lived a life of opulence my son could never give you."

Beth nodded, knowing what the woman said was true and how she'd faced so much prejudice from everyone at the ranch who thought she knew nothing and could never learn. But she'd showed them.

Ethan's mother sighed. "But you have one trait I admire so much and know it's what's proven everyone wrong. You're as stubborn as I am and determined to show you can learn. You'll make my son an excellent wife."

"Yes, ma'am," Beth said, knowing it was true.

"I'm so glad you're here," Mama Fraser said, pulling Beth in for a hug.

Beth's throat clogged with tears. The woman she thought would never see her as worthy for her beloved son was telling her she was accepted and loved, and now Beth was going to destroy that trust by leaving on the Sunday morning train to Chicago. Her chest felt like it would explode from the pain, yet she had to go. She didn't belong here.

"I can see my son falling in love with you before my eyes, and let me just say I'm so happy you're his wife. You've shown us all that anything is possible and reminded us not to judge others by their circumstances. I'm so happy to call you my daughter."

Biting her lip to keep from sobbing, Beth felt a tear trickle down her cheek. She was leaving when she'd finally been accepted, and more importantly, her husband was falling in love with her. Quickly swiping away the tear, she gave her mother-in-law a squeeze.

"Thank you. That means a lot. I have to tell you I think being here has forced me to grow up and learn so many things about life and who I am."

Her mother-in-law chuckled. "Honey, that's what marriage does to a girl. Forces her to grow up and put away those childish dreams. Now, here comes my good-looking son. You two have a good time tonight."

Beth stood and faced her husband as he walked up beside her. He grabbed her arm, pulling her out onto the dance floor for a waltz.

"Usually a gentleman asks a lady for a dance," she reminded him.

"Not with his wife. The only gentleman dancing with you is me," he said, pulling her in closer and holding her tight. "In fact, we may not last long at this dance tonight."

A grin spread across his face, and she knew exactly what he had in mind. A blush bloomed on her cheeks, yet she couldn't deny that the thought of spending one last night in Ethan's arms was exciting. Right now, she couldn't deny him anything because after tomorrow, they would be married in name only, and he would hate her.

That thought troubled her more than she cared to think about.

"We're here to dance," she said.

"And that's what we're doing. But I'm thinking about a different kind of dance between me and you without all these people around," he said low in her ear, his breath sending tremors through her.

Why was Ethan the only man who'd ever created these types of feelings in her? Just the woodsy smell of him was enough to have her thinking of tangled sheets and their slick bodies touching.

"Mr. Fraser, you are a scoundrel," she said swallowing hard.

"Only with my wife and then I can be both her hero and her scoundrel," he said, his torso brushing against her.

"Ethan," she squealed. "That's not proper."

Yet, the mere touch of him against her was enough to cause her breath to speed up like she was running a race. Her heart was pounding, and she wanted him to touch her more…everywhere.

He chuckled. "That's why I think we should just leave now and go to the hotel."

"No. Everyone will know where we're going."

"And you don't think every man who is married here tonight is itching for a way to get his woman alone, so he can spend some time in her arms?"

Beth glanced around the room, pretending to take notice of everyone. "Maybe. But I'm sure every woman here is playing coy, trying to spend a little more time talking to her neighbors, flirting with her husband, feeling his arms around her on the dance floor, before she lets him whisk her away. It's the anticipation."

"How much time do you need?" he asked.

She laughed. "We've only been here an hour."

"That's plenty long enough. We have that nice big hotel room with a comfortable bed waiting on us."

Reaching up, she let her fingers trail down his cheek, noting the way his brown eyes widened and darkened at the same time. She'd learned at an early age how she could affect men but never like with Ethan, and the strange thing was she only wanted Ethan.

The music came to a halt, and everyone clapped for the musicians. A Virginia reel was announced, and a line formed quickly with Beth and Ethan as the head couple. As they swung with the right shoulder, he shouted in her ear, "We could be naked in that big bed."

She laughed at him, as his words sent a thrill down her spine.

When they swung with the left shoulder, he whispered, "I could be kissing your soft skin."

"Ethan," she said, her voice sounding more whispery than demanding. The man was being incorrigible, yet his words were affecting her body in ways she'd never imagined.

When they slid down the line, their hands touching, she leaned close to him and said, "I could be running my hands over your strong muscles." Two could play this teasing game.

He groaned and she smiled at him, happy to know she affected him as much as he did her.

When they do-si-doed, he leaned in close. "I love the way you smell tonight, Mrs. Fraser. A mixture of seduction and sweetness."

As they slid down the line again, she stared into his gaze, unable to look away. "It's all natural," she said. "But you, you smell of man and leather and that delicious smell of just you."

When they were no longer the main couple, they continued dancing, but Beth could hardly wait for the dance to end. Five couples were behind them, and it took what seemed like forever.

Finally, the last couple held their arms up, and the rest of the couples promenaded through their outstretched arms, and the music came to a halt.

Breathless and warm, she glanced over at her husband and yawned. "I'm feeling tired. It might be time to call it a night."

"I thought you'd never say so," he said, grabbing her by the arm and pulling her through the crowd.

They waved goodbye to his mother and brothers, and Beth felt a wrenching in her heart. She'd never see any of these people again, and they would always remember her for being the woman who'd left Ethan. They would hate her, and right now, she didn't know if she could blame them.

While walking through the door, her husband turned back and gave her such a warm smile she quickly pushed her dark thoughts away. Tonight, she wanted to concentrate on Ethan. Nothing else, except the two of them. There would be months ahead of her to think about her decision, but tonight belonged to her husband.

∼

Ethan had known his wife was beautiful, but seeing her tonight all decked out in the dress Olivia and his mother had altered for the dance made him realize he was a very lucky man. She was the prettiest gal there tonight. He'd had eyes only for her, and he'd had a hard time refraining from picking her up and carrying her out the door.

They'd been married less than two months, but in that time, she'd changed and grown and dragged him kicking and screaming along with her. She'd come to him a young woman who was used to being waited on with servants, and he'd watched her evolve into a woman he was proud to call his wife. Now she was a woman who could take charge. If he gave her a job, it would get done.

And while she was changing, he'd realized with each day, he was falling in love with her. Now he couldn't imagine his life without her by his side, every step of the way.

Tonight would be a celebration of their joining. They would soon have a home and before long, children pitter-pattering through the house, with him and Beth giving chase. He couldn't wait for the day they learned Beth was with child, and he hoped to make it happen this very night. But if not tonight, then very soon.

Stepping out into the cool night air, he placed her hand on his arm. "Look, it's a full moon."

She smiled at him. "All I'm looking at is you."

He pulled her tightly to him as they walked down the wooden sidewalk toward the hotel. "If you keep talking like that, we'll be running to that hotel room."

"We're almost running now," she said.

He grinned at her, knowing it was true. "That's because I can't wait to get you behind closed doors."

"And what pray tell do you plan on doing to me?"

"I'm going to ravish your sweet, beautiful body until you're begging me to stop."

"Oh, Mr. Fraser," she said. "Maybe we should walk a little quicker."

They'd never bantered sexually before. Never had they felt comfortable enough to tease one another, and he couldn't wait to see if this easiness carried over to their bedroom. He hoped it would because he was looking forward to tonight.

"You know I think we should eat dinner somewhere before we go to the hotel. I think I'm starving," she said, her hazel eyes glittering with mischief.

Oh mercy, he hoped she was teasing because he didn't know if he could wait much longer. It seemed like forever since they'd made love, and he wanted her so badly he was near bursting.

Placing his mouth next to her ear, he nuzzled her neck and earlobe, his tongue sliding across her ear. A shiver rippled through her, and he smiled, knowing he was affecting her as much as she was him.

"I'll wake up the cook at the dinner," he said, nipping her earlobe with his teeth.

"Never mind, I'm not hungry for food," she said, her voice whispery soft like she was breathless.

They reached the door of the hotel, and he pulled it open for her. He led her up to their room on the second floor, the sexual suspense building like a gathering storm that was about to be unleashed.

Putting the key in the lock, he slowly turned it, opened the door, and turned to glance at her, relishing the anticipation. She was biting her lip, her eyes wide with expectation and something that looked like desire. He stood there for a moment, letting them both anticipate what was about to happen before he would release the hunger for his wife raging through him.

She met his gaze head on, her breathing quick and shallow. She wanted this as much as he did, and her desire sent him over the edge. He walked into the room, pulling her inside, and shut the door. As soon as the lock clicked behind him, he pushed her up against the wooden panel, his body covering hers, pressing into her soft voluptuous curves, his rock-solid erection snug against her womanly mound, his mouth coming down hard against hers.

She moaned, deep in her throat, and he relished the sound. While his lips never left hers as he caressed her sweet mouth, his hands were busy working the buttons at the back of her dress, needing to reach her skin, to feel that soft, satiny flesh beneath his fingertips.

Abruptly, she broke the seal of their mouths and began to frantically work the buttons on his shirt. "I want to run my hands over your chest."

"Yes," he whispered, barely able to talk, his need for her so great.

When he finished undoing her buttons, he gently shoved the beautiful dress down to the floor. Then he reached for her chemise. Quickly, he pulled it over her head and pushed away her pantaloons, leaving her in her stockings.

Her fingertips trailed from his neck down to his waist, where she unbuttoned his pants. He reached down and pulled off his boots and socks. As he thrust his pants to the floor, she slid his shirt off his shoulders. He watched as she rolled down her stockings. Then they were standing there in front of the wooden door naked, breathing hard and staring at one another.

Simultaneously, they swayed toward one another, reaching out at the same time, as he pulled her mouth to his, wanting to feel her beautiful lips against his. A moan filled the air, and he was shocked to realize the sound came from him as he crushed her mouth beneath his own, hunger guiding and filling him.

Beth was his wife, his woman, and tonight, he would make her his own. Tonight, he would worship her body and show her how she had stolen his heart, and hopefully, he would forge his heart with hers. He loved this woman, his wife, his love, and tonight, he planned on showing her how much.

Breaking the seal of their lips, he leaned his forehead against hers. "Do you know how much I want you?"

"I think so," she said, her voice soft, her breath whispery.

"No one has ever made me feel like you do. No one has made me want to fight heaven and earth to be with you," he promised as he walked backwards to the bed in the center of the room.

A shiver went through her.

"Are you cold? Let me warm you." He pulled her down with him to the bed.

"I'm not cold. I'm hot with need for you," she said, her fingertips running down his chest, his stomach, to his manhood. She wrapped her hand around him, and he groaned with pleasure. He felt full to bursting with need for her as she stroked him.

"Then let me fix that for you because I ache with desire for you," he said as he gripped her head, holding her mouth hostage, his fingers tangling in her hair, not letting her escape his kiss.

Then he slid his hands down her neck to her shoulders and further down until he reached her chest. Cupping her pale globes, he released her mouth from his and leaned down to lift the soft weight of her breast to his lips. Gently, he tugged on her nipple, sucking as much of her into his mouth as he could, as she bucked wildly against him, moaning deep in her throat. Her breathing was ragged as her hands moved to his head, trapping him against her breasts as she strained, trying to give him more access to her body.

He moved his hand down her body, skimming over her flat stomach, down until he touched her womanly folds, and she cried out his name.

Pulling his mouth off of her breast, he watched as passion filled her eyes, and she gazed at him with longing.

"Damn, you feel like silk," he said as he parted her folds and delved inside her. Slowly, he stroked her, watching her face change. Her fingers gripped the quilt as his fingers brought her pleasure. Honey flowed, a natural lubricant that told him he was doing something right. Her body tightened around him, and she cried out, shuddering as her passion-filled eyes stared straight into his soul.

Smiling, he parted her legs with his. Her body fit perfectly against him, her breasts touching his chest, her hips supporting him, his manhood nestled between the juncture of her thighs, right where he belonged. Unable to hold back any longer, he entered her in a single swift movement. This woman, his wife, his lover, filled him with passion like no one else. And he'd waited as long as possible. But no more.

"You feel wonderful," she whispered into his ear. "Filling me up like this."

"Beth," he whispered. "This is where I belong. Inside of you, my wife."

Staring into her eyes, he felt they were connected as one as he moved inside her, stroking her, loving her. Clutching his back, she clung to him as they rode the waves of passion together, holding onto to one another

Love filled his heart, and he knew he would give Beth the sun, the moon, and the stars if he could. When they married, he hadn't really wanted her. Then she'd showed him how lonely his life had been, and she'd filled it with joy and love and made him into a man. A better man who cared about others, a man who no longer knew how to live without her.

This woman had taken on the challenges of living on the ranch and beat them, even while they'd humbled her. And he adored her strength and perseverance. She was everything he wanted, and he'd spend the rest of his days showing her his love, protecting and honoring her.

A tightening spiral of pleasure filled him, and as much as he wished he could last longer, he couldn't.

"Ethan!" Beth called out just as he felt her body convulsing with pleasure.

His manhood tightened and swelled within her. With a guttural cry, he slammed into her body, shuddering his release. No matter what happened in their future, he would always remember tonight as the night he'd given her his heart. Something he'd never done with a woman before, and he was glad he'd waited until Beth was thrust into his life.

His heart was pounding, his breathing heavy, as he rolled them to their sides, pulling her snug against his body. She looked up at him, and he reached down and kissed her on the lips.

"I love you, Beth. You've made my life a better place and me a better man. I never expected to feel these emotions, but I love you with all my heart and soul. I'm yours until I take my last breath."

She laid her head on his chest and squeezed him hard. "Oh, Ethan."

Chapter Fourteen

Beth laid awake all night, listening to her husband breathe, the sound of his heart beating against her chest, staring at the way his hair curled at his nape. These were things she'd never forget, and as she watched the sun rise in the eastern sky, she questioned her decision.

Last night Ethan had confessed his love, shattering her heart. No man had ever told her he loved her. Henry had never professed love for her. In fact, he'd barely spent time with her, treating her more like a child than an equal. But she wouldn't be returning to Henry. She'd be returning to her father. And even that decision she questioned.

She'd been gone six weeks. If he'd wanted to find her, he would have by now. And when she returned, would he welcome her home with open arms and still let her live there? What if he told her to get out? What would she do then?

But the plan had always been to leave once she obtained the marriage license, which Ethan had gotten yesterday. There was no reason to stay, except she suddenly was questioning everything.

As the sun rose, she quietly left the bed and dressed, hoping to leave before Ethan awakened. They'd made love into the early morning hours, cherishing each other's bodies. It was her last hours with him, and she'd given everything of herself to him, and he'd given her his heart. And now she was going to break it.

Quickly, she penned him a note.

Dearest Ethan,

When I came here, I never expected to stay. My intent was to marry then leave. Today, I return to Chicago a married woman. I have no intentions of annulling our marriage or even obtaining a divorce. These past six weeks have been the best weeks of my life, and I've learned so much from you and your family.

You, dear husband, have been extremely kind and gracious to me. You've helped me learn so much about myself and my shortcomings.

I would stay, but my place is in Chicago, and yours is here in the mountains. Again, I thank you for everything you've done for me, and I'm sorry I can't stay.

Beth

Why did she feel like she was leaving something out? Something so important.

Ethan rolled over and stretched, and for a moment, she feared he would awaken, but then he fell back into a deep slumber. She sighed with relief and regret.

What if she was making the biggest mistake of her life? What if she was leaving the best man she'd ever met? But what if she didn't return to the place she belonged?

She had to go back. She had to see her father and clear her good name. Once everyone in Chicago learned the real reason she'd deserted the wedding, she would be welcomed with open arms. She'd be praised for learning the truth and acting so courageously. But did her society friends' opinions really matter?

Quickly, before she could change her mind, she grabbed her valise and reticule, placed the note on the table where he would find it, and walked out the door, shutting it quietly behind her.

For just a moment, she leaned against the door, tears in her eyes as she thought of last night. Her husband was a magnificent man who had given her a taste of being a real wife.

Now, she would return to Chicago as a married woman to show her former fiancé that he shouldn't have trifled with her affections.

~

Ethan rolled over blindly, reaching out, hoping to find Beth still in bed with him. They'd not gone to sleep until the wee hours of the morning, and he'd wanted to waken his bride with another round of lovemaking before they dressed and headed back to the ranch. If he'd known Beth would open up to him so well in a hotel room, he would have ridden through a snowstorm to get them to Angel Springs much earlier in their marriage.

When his hand didn't find her sweet body, he opened his eyes and glanced around the room. It was empty. Sitting up in bed, he thought maybe she'd gone downstairs to get them coffee and was going to surprise him. But then he glanced over to the table, where she'd put her valise and noticed it was gone. Everything of hers was gone.

Jumping out of bed, he pulled on his pants and grabbed his shirt. How in the hell had the woman snuck out of the room without him hearing her? And what in tarnation was she doing?

They were married. He'd given her the license yesterday, for better or worse until death parted them.

And after last night, he'd thought she'd soon be telling him she loved him. He was a little shocked she hadn't said the words after the passion they'd shared. The emotion had been shining from her eyes, unless he'd just been stupid and imagined it.

Glancing around the room, he couldn't find his socks. Finally, he just grabbed his boots and shoved in his feet.

He didn't know what was going on, but he was going to find Beth. Before last night, he wouldn't have been surprised if she'd tried to catch the train back to Chicago. But after they'd made love, he felt everything had changed. They'd joined their hearts and souls with their lovemaking, and he would be shocked if she left him now.

Regardless, she was his wife. He would get her back.

Grabbing his hat off the table, it was then he saw the note.

Picking it up, he read the terse explanation she'd left him. Now, he knew exactly where she was headed. She was catching the nine o'clock train to Chicago. She was going home.

He glanced at his pocket watch. He had five minutes to stop her.

"Damn," he said and ran out of the room. Maybe the train would be late. He had to stop her, or he'd find himself making an unscheduled trip to Chicago.

~

Beth walked onto the train and took a seat. She was going home. Glancing out the window, she stared at the town that had changed her life, the place where she'd finally grown up and gotten a taste of how most people lived.

The image of Ethan came into her mind, and tears clogged her throat. The man had been nothing but good to her. He'd helped her, he'd taken the time to show her how to do things, he'd treated her like she was smart, and he'd been patient with her. No one had ever been as tender and caring as he had, and now she was leaving him behind.

And why? Because she wanted to prove to people who had never cared about her nor loved her like he did that her ex-fiancé was the one to blame for her running from a wedding that was doomed from the start?

She was going to take a chance and leave behind a man she'd fallen in love with just to prove she was right? Was she crazy?

"All aboard!" the conductor called, pulling in the step then closing the doors.

"Wait!" she cried. She couldn't leave. She didn't give a hoot about what the people in Chicago thought. If they were concerned for her, they would have come after her. All she cared about and who she loved was right here in Angel Springs, Colorado.

Grabbing her reticule and her valise, she jumped up out of her seat as people stared.

"Miss, the train is leaving."

"I'm not going. Everything I want is right here. I'm not going back," she said and stepped off the train.

As soon as her feet touched the ground, the train began rolling. Standing there on the platform, she started to cry. She'd almost left him. She'd almost run away from the man who she loved with all her heart and soul, the man she couldn't live without, all because of her dang pride.

The train gathered steam as it pulled out of the station. As she watched it go, she felt like the old Beth was still on that train riding out of town. The rich society girl was heading back to Chicago, and the new Beth who was a wife and hopefully soon a mother was just beginning her life.

This Beth, the real Beth, couldn't wait to find Ethan and tell him what she'd discovered. How much she loved him and wanted to be his wife.

When the last car left the station, and the tracks cleared. She saw him.

He was standing on the other side of the tracks, staring dejectedly at the disappearing train.

"Ethan!" she cried.

He glanced up and started running toward her.

She hurried as fast as her dress would allow toward the man she loved. Her husband.

"Beth," he said, grabbing her to him. "I thought you were on that train."

She reached up to caress his face. "I was. But I couldn't go. I couldn't leave you. I love you, Ethan Fraser. I love you more than you will ever know."

He kissed her lips and wrapped his arms tighter around her. "Oh, Beth. I've been waiting to hear you say those words."

She pulled back. "I need to be honest with you and promise you that from this day forward I will always be truthful with you."

Ethan frowned down at her, but he didn't let her go. "Okay."

"Since the day I married you, I've planned on leaving, hopefully with the marriage license, but even without it, I'd planned to return to Chicago. Yesterday, you gave me that license."

"I did."

"But you see what I hadn't counted on was falling in love with you. I wanted to return to Chicago and show my father and my former fiancé that it was too late. That I already had a husband, and they couldn't make me marry Henry." She was standing near the railroad tracks, gazing up at the man she loved, needing him to understand her desperation, the reasons for her actions, and why she would never again leave him.

"Why did you run from your first wedding, Beth? You've never told me the real reason."

She hung her head, and a shudder went through her at the image. "I saw Henry kissing a man. It was a passionate kiss, much better than the pecks on the cheek he gave me. I told my father, and he said I was mistaken. I was making stuff up because I had pre-wedding jitters. I didn't, Ethan. I didn't love Henry, but I realized he only wanted our marriage as a front."

Ethan hugged her closer to him. "If you hadn't run, you wouldn't have come to Colorado. I wouldn't have married you. I don't care about Henry as long as you don't love him."

"I love you, Ethan. I may not be the best wife for you, but I will stand by you and love you all of my days here on this earth and even into the next life. You're the man for me."

Ethan's mouth crashed down on hers in a punishing kiss that almost left her faint. She held onto him, letting him wreak havoc on her senses, wishing they weren't standing at the railroad but were back at the hotel.

Finally, he let her go. "Don't ever leave me again, Beth."

She reached up and touched her fingers to his lips. "I won't, Ethan. I want to be your wife."

"Let's go home, Mrs. Fraser."

"I can't wait to get there, Mr. Fraser. Do you think the animals will be okay listening to us all night long up in the loft?"

He laughed and picked up her valise. "After hearing us all night, I wouldn't be surprised if there are lots of baby animals this spring."

Chapter Fifteen

June 1881

Beth stood outside in the summer sunshine, the cool mountain breeze blowing tendrils of hair away from her face. The sound of hammers banging on lumber kept her from her chores as she watched the progress on the home they were building.

"Ethan, it's lunchtime!" she called.

He stopped, wiped the sweat from his brow, and motioned for the men to come down from the rafters. It wasn't a huge house, but there was plenty of space to add on, and they'd designed the plans for the growing family they soon hoped to have.

"Spunky, how are you?" she asked the man whose face she'd smashed a cake into. They were now good friends, and he often teased her about her temper.

"Doing fine, Mrs. Fraser. Is there cake for lunch?"

"You're favorite. Strawberry."

"Get out of my way," he said and ran toward the bunkhouse, where lunch was being served.

Today was the day Beth had chosen to tell Ethan her news. She'd been waiting until she was certain, but her sisters-in-law all agreed. It was time.

When all the men had left the area, she walked up to Ethan. "Honey, I need you to explain something to me again."

He took a sip of water from the bucket and glanced at her. "What?"

"Tell me again where the extra bedrooms are going to be located in the new house? I know where our bedroom is, but show me where the two extra are located."

"Beth, you're not a dumb woman. We've been over this several times."

She smiled, hoping she wasn't giving away her surprise, but she wanted him to show her. Then she would tell him her news. "I know, but I want to make certain. Show me in the house."

He took her hand and led her into the structure. "This room is the parlor, here is the kitchen, and these two rooms on this side of the house are the extra bedrooms."

"Okay. I just wanted to make sure the nursery would be close enough I could hear the baby cry."

He glanced at her, his brown eyes widening. She giggled as he stared at her, the realization penetrating. "Are you expecting?"

"I think so," she said laughing. "Baby Fraser should arrive sometime around the first of the year."

Pulling her into his arms, he lifted her and spun her around. "I'm so excited."

"Me too," she said, loving her husband's arms around her.

"Are you feeling okay?" he asked, suddenly putting her back on the ground.

"I feel great," she said. "I'm so happy, Ethan." She hugged him to her. "With you as my husband and now our first child, I couldn't be any happier."

She held onto her husband, knowing this was where she belonged. She didn't think she'd ever grow tired of the way he loved her.

"Happier than when your father came to visit?"

She laughed out loud at the memory of her father showing up one day and staying for a whole two days. While she was glad they had reconciled, she knew she would seldom see or hear from him any longer. And it was okay. Her life was here in Angel Springs, Colorado, with the man who had shown her real love.

"You know the answer to that, Papa Fraser. Now let's go have lunch. I'm feeling a little hungry."

"I love you, Beth."

"I love you so much, Ethan, and I love this child we created."

Thank You For Reading!

Dear Reader,

Thanks for reading *Ethan*. I hope you enjoyed this family as much as all the authors did. Special thanks to Caroline Clemmons, Callie Hutton, Cynthia Woolf for working so hard to produce these books. We quickly discovered that writing a family from each of our perspectives was challenging.

As always, if you're inclined, please leave a review. Whether or not you loved the book or hated it,-I'd enjoy your feedback. Reviews are difficult to obtain and have the power to make or break a book.

If you enjoy western historical authors, please join the Pioneer Hearts group on Facebook. This is a fabulous group of readers and authors who enjoy westerns. We have lots of fun and there is always something going on.

Sign up for my newsletter if you'd like to learn about my new releases before everyone else.

Thanks for venturing into my world and may I see you here again soon.

Yours in Drama, Divas, Bad Boys and Romance!
Sincerely,
Sylvia McDaniel

Books by Sylvia McDaniel

Contemporary Romance

Standalones
The Reluctant Santa
My Sister's Boyfriend
The Wanted Bride
The Relationship Coach
Her Christmas Lie
Secrets, Lies, and Online Dating
Paying for the Past
Cupid's Revenge

Anthologies
Kisses, Laughter & Love
Christmas with you

Collaborative Series

Magic, New Mexico
Touch of Decadence

Western Historicals

Standalones
A Hero's Heart
A Scarlet Bride
Second Chance Cowboy

The Cuvier Women
Wronged
Betrayed
Beguiled

Lipstick and Lead
Desperate
Deadly
Dangerous
Daring
Determined
Deceived

Scandalous Suffragettes
Abigail
Bella
Callie
Faith

The Burnett Brides
The Rancher Takes a Bride
The Outlaw Takes a Bride
The Marshal Takes a Bride
The Christmas Bride

Anthologies
Wild Western Women
Courting the West
Wild Western Women Ride Again

Collaborative Series

The Surprise Brides
Ethan

American Mail Order Brides
Katie

About the Author

Sylvia McDaniel is a best-selling, award-winning author of historical romance and contemporary romance novels. Known for her sweet, funny, family-oriented romances, Sylvia is the author of The Burnett Brides, a western historical western series, The Cuvier Widows, a Louisiana historical series, and several short contemporary romances.

She is the former President of the Dallas Area Romance Authors, a member of the Romance Writers of America®, and a member of Novelists Inc. Her novel, A Hero's Heart, was a 1996 Golden Heart Finalist. Several other books have placed or won in the San Antonio Romance Authors Contest and the LERA Contest, and she was a Golden Network Finalist.

Married for nearly twenty years to her best friend, they have two dachshunds that are beyond spoiled and a good-looking, grown son who thinks there's no place like home. She loves gardening, shopping, knitting, and football (Cowboys and Bronco's fan), but not necessarily in that order.

Look for her the first Tuesday of every month at the Plotting Princesses blogspot, and be sure to sign up for her newsletter to learn about new releases and contests. Every month a new subscriber is entered into a drawing for a free book!

She can be found online at: www.sylviamcdaniel.com or on Facebook. You can write to Sylvia at P.O. Box 2542, Coppell, TX 75019.

relationship. When she realizes he doesn't remember the breakup, she thinks that life has given her a second chance with the man she loves. At least until his memory returns.

Can a wedding and Christmas heal Tyler and give Kelsey the strength she needs to be a military wife? Can a soldier forgive the girl he loves when she sends him a Dear John letter?

Sneak Peek into Her Christmas Lie

Losing his memory had some advantages, but mainly it created problems. Like how could he forget where Kelsey Johnson, his fiancée, lived? Of course, she'd moved here during the months he liked to call the dark days. He couldn't remember a thing from March to November because a roadside bomb in Kabul had obliterated his Humvee, giving him a near death experience and a one month hospital stay in Germany. All courtesy of Afghan insurgents.

Marine Second Lieutenant Tyler Ferguson shifted restlessly in the back seat of the cab. How would Kelsey react when she saw the bandage on his head and the wound in his leg, which was better, but far from healed? He'd been lucky. His driver, Sargent George McDonald didn't fare as well and he hated that. They'd become friends as he drove him around the desert rebuilding the infrastructure so his fellow marines could communicate and do recon work.

He'd been gone nine months, and for the last two, he'd had no communication with Kelsey. She must be worried sick. Him showing up unannounced, he hoped was a great surprise. He couldn't wait to gaze into her green eyes and let his fingers comb through her silken red curls.

Would it be rude, just to pick her up and carry her straight into the bedroom? He'd missed her so much, his heart ached as the miles separating them shrunk. It'd been so long since he'd felt her warm, loving arms around him.

Just the thought of seeing her, brought tears to his eyes. For a while he'd thought he'd never see her again. But finally his body had responded to the doctors' treatments and then they'd delivered the bad news.

Maybe he'd lost more than just days in a hospital. Maybe he'd lost months, possibly forever, but his mind was working, his body was healing and even his leg was better. He had a lot to be thankful for.

So he couldn't remember the last nine months. The blast seemed to sear away the time he'd been in Afghanistan and frankly, he was okay with that as long as he could remember today and yesterday and every day going forward. Especially if it was spent with the woman he loved.

Snow fell softly as they drove through the Denver, Colorado neighborhood. He'd found her address on Google and given it to the driver. The cab pulled to a stop and he gingerly stepped out, hoping his bad leg held. Paying the driver, he said, "Thanks, man."

"Good luck, soldier," the cab driver said.

Tyler felt a grin spread across his face. Yanking off his cap, he pulled out the Santa hat he'd bought in the airport. With flowers in one hand, his duffle bag in the other, he limped up the sidewalk to the front door.

The home looked inviting, a wide wooden porch, with patio chairs beneath the overhang eves. The neighborhood was an older, more settled type of homeowner. The kind of place with families and dogs and backyard barbecues. The only problem was Kelsey hadn't decorated for Christmas which surprised him. She loved the holiday season and always decked the house from the inside out.

With trembling fingers, he rang the bell and waited impatiently. Just when he was ready to give up, he heard the door locks being pulled back. Anticipation at seeing the woman he loved, tore at his rapidly beating heart. This point in time seemed to drag clear into next week. When she pulled back the wooden door, he opened his arms wide. "Merry Christmas!"

For a moment, Kelsey stared at him in shock and then she came outside. Gently, she reached up and put her hand to his head. He'd waited so long for her loving touch...a whole four weeks, but he knew it'd been longer. "You're hurt."

"Yeah, I had a little meeting with a roadside bomb. But the insurgents didn't live to tell about the destruction they'd caused." The doctors had refused to let him remove the bandage around his head until after the next appointment.

"Tyler," she whispered her voice choked.

Why wasn't she kissing him? Sure, he probably looked worse than he felt, but since the day of the bombing, he'd dreamed about her lips moving against his.

"Are you badly injured?" she asked.

"A little memory loss." He laughed and shrugged, wanting only to kiss her. "I've been anticipating your mouth and all you want to talk about is how badly hurt I am?"

Sweeping her into his arms, he pulled her body in close to him. His lips came crashing down on hers in a kiss that he'd been waiting for. A kiss filled with promises of love and devotion and assurances of nights of mind-blowing sex. He craved some between the sheets action with his woman in a major way.

Her arms slowly wound around him, as she gave herself over to the demands of his mouth. He wanted her as close as he could get her without doing the tango right here on her porch, under the stars, while the neighbors watched.

She stepped out of his arms and stared at him, her emerald eyes shimmering with tears. "Come in, Tyler, we need to talk."

www.ingramcontent.com/pod-product-compliance
Lightning Source LLC
Chambersburg PA
CBHW070948190726
48292CB00004B/1385